Jesus Gnosis

Story of Simon

By Philip

T0142727

Thomas Ragland

Order this book online at www.trafford.com
or email orders@trafford.com

Most Trafford titles are also available at major online book retailers.

Note for Librarians: A cataloguing record for this book is available from Library
and Archives Canada at www.collectionscanada.ca/amicus/index-e.html

Printed in Victoria, BC, Canada.

ISBN: 9781-4269-136-5-5

*Our mission is to efficiently provide the world's finest, most comprehensive
book publishing service, enabling every author to experience success.
To find out how to publish your book, your way, and have it available
worldwide, visit us online at www.trafford.com*

Trafford rev. 08/10/09

 www.trafford.com

North America & international
toll-free: 1 888 232 4444 (USA & Canada)
phone: 250 383 6864 ♦ fax: 250 383 6804 ♦ email: info@trafford.com

10 9 8 7 6 5 4 3 2 1

Adventures

Bethsaida

Philip saith unto him, Lord, shew us the Father, and it sufficeth us. Jesus saith unto him, Have I been so long time with you, and yet hast thou not known me, Philip? he that hath seen me hath seen the Father; and how sayest thou then, Shew us the Father? Believest thou not that I am in the Father, and the Father in me? the words that I speak unto you I speak not of myself: but the Father that dwelleth in me, he doeth the works.[1]

To speak certain words, to think certain thoughts, to dream certain dreams, to accomplish certain tasks, involves a direct-connect into what some call the Father, into What Is, into the ultimate Source in a way that is unfiltered by the limited mindsets of normal human thought. When you lift this veil and peer into this vision, silence the distractions and tune into this channel, what you then stand for and speak and do captures an essence that is beyond the normal. You come to know that which cannot be known, see connections that others do not see, describe in words that which cannot be described, and experience things that are labeled as miracles.

This is a story about a man who lived close to me. Sometimes you are fortunate enough to accidentally, or is it by some predestined fate, stumble across experiences and experiencers that are so vivid, so pronounced, so real in a way that you can't really describe. Simon's experiences were like this. My experiences were like this, but Simon had taken it to an entirely different level. I think it had to do with his mother-in-law, but I'm getting ahead of the story.

Some things you have to become before you can see what is really going on. These things are difficult to explain to those who haven't experienced them. How can you be taught to see what is invisible to you? How can you be taught to become that which is impossible for you? To those who have not, what little they encounter will immediately fall away and be lost.[2] To those who have a little, more will come and be collected, and the more that is collected the more will become apparent. Jesus is like this, and I wish I could explain it all in simpler terms. Jesus is simple once you know, but as to how to get to know, that is the question.

Such an ability to direct-connect to something that is real and not just imagined, to something transformational and not just resting on the hopes of blind faith in dogmatic promises, would be sought out, even by people vastly different. Direct experience transcends culture and

---

[1] John 14:8-10

[2] Matthew 25:29 , Matthew 13:12

language. If there is Something Real to experience, it must be bigger than capable of being contained by one religion, by one small set of people. If there are miracles and signs, transformed lives, connected intuitions and observed synchronicities, and a sense of connection to something that ties us all together and changes the very focus of our identity, then there will be those who appreciate and run after such a metaphysical force. The force in this story is called Jesus, an entity that lies somewhere between God and humanity, between natural and supernatural, between real and dreamed, touched and encountered in visions.

> And there were certain Greeks among them that came up to worship at the feast: The same came therefore to Philip, which was of Bethsaida of Galilee, and desired him, saying, Sir, we would see Jesus.[3]
>
> Then Simon himself believed also: and when he was baptized, he continued with Philip, and wondered, beholding the miracles and signs which were done.[4]

Bethsaida is my hometown.[5] My name is Philip. I was one of the first to encounter Jesus. The people I knew thought I'd lost it. What good can come of such wild fantasy delusions? Well, it is just something you have to experience for yourself. The story is not about me. I'm a bit too practical to think outside of box of convention. Or at least I was back then. Priests should be priests, philosophers should be philosophers, merchants should be merchants. I dealt in horses. There was this one time that there was this totally wild untamable horse that no one could ride.[6] I had her tied up by the side of the house. I saw Jesus walking down the street plain as day, but glowing and somehow mysteriously of a different dimension. I didn't know he was Jesus at the time. That was before Simon explained him to me. I did know that he was something other than just a normal man. I don't know how to explain it any better. He sat on the wild horse and gently and slowly rode down the street on her. Simon appeared out of nowhere and turned to me and simply said, the Master needs her and will bring her back shortly. I didn't know what to say. Simon was the older brother of my best friend Andy. We had grown up together and up until recently, Simon had been just one of the boys. This Jesus experience had changed him. I will have to admit that it has changed me too. This story is about Simon. It is about him because of all of us he changed the most and saw the most and of all of us laid more of a foundation for future generations to share in the Jesus experience.

---

[3] John 12:20-21

[4] Acts 8:13

[5] John 1:44

[6] John 12:14

My part in this is that I'm a storyteller with a hope a bit of horse sense. The subject doesn't lend itself well to keeping a completely level head, but it is not all mindless invented speculation either.

I guess it all began at a wedding.[7] My friend Andy's brother was getting married. The girl came from a rich family, well, rich for Bethsaida. They owned the pottery shop, an old store that had been there for years. Martha, the bride, had taken over the business after her father died and her mother had gotten sick and bed ridden. Because the mother could not leave the shop, but lived in one of the rooms in the back, the wedding was in the store. They had filled several custom made pots with wine for the celebration. The party got to be more than they anticipated and the wine had run out. The mother called for Simon, the groom, to come and speak with her. She said with a weak voice for him to take some of the empty pots and fill them up with water. What use is that, Simon thought out loud. Just humor an old lady, Simon's new mother-in-law answered. You are the man of the family now, you have to be my rock, she added. He didn't know quite what to make of her. She seemed a bit odd. But he was truly in love with Martha and would put up with her mother's strange ways. In the end, he did what he was instructed and filled up a couple of empty jars with water. Since the wine was out, some of the guests began to get refills from these jars with water and they all began to talk about how good the wine was. Someone noted that most people serve the good stuff first and then bring out the cheap stuff after everyone's good and drunk, but at this party they saved the best for last. Simon didn't know what to think. He turned to his mother-in-law and she was sitting there with a serene smile and a far away bliss on her face.

It's like those childhood memory flashes that zap into focus, recalled by some random seemingly unrelated sight, or a déjà vu moment of walking down a familiar path, a feeling of being included on a great secret that the rest of the world is not in on, hearing the voices that are only imagined and yet more real than the sound coming out of a busy marketplace. It is a memory of being alive, of living in the moment, of having it all make sense and be so simple. It is a richness that doesn't cost anything and can't be bought. It is a reality that can't be encapsulated, held prisoner in a tower, chained down enough to draw its portrait. It can't really be described to anyone who hasn't experienced it firsthand. Words fail. Paintings cannot capture the patterns. Music can't keep up with its ever-changing rhythms and textures. Empathic waves of intuitively knowing why the bird in the tree is singing, why the white fluffy clouds are blowing across the otherwise clear blue sky. What used to be commonplace is now grasped on the border of fleeting moments of those childhood memory flashes, reminding this aging man that all of his dreams have not yet withered.

---

[7] John 2:1-11

Jesus   Gnosis   3

Some things that seem so real are just a product of us being conditioned to see things a certain way, with this overlaid filter of prejudices and phobias, habits and traditions. But there are some things that seem so unreal that have a sense of presence and value that linger even in the context of being surrounding by other people who have not had, or perhaps cannot have, the same experience. When you see the synchronicities play out in events and the placement of people at the exact right place and the exact right time, and against all odds everything works out, you have to wonder about how it happens. For all the talk of gods and goddesses, ancestors and angels, the how of it remains but speculation, labels placed on the mystery of how it works. There is no question of "that" it works, just "how" and what it all means. The same with intuitively knowing that something is about to happen -- where does it come from? What connects us all?

Simon liked to get away from town and take walks alone, get away and think.[8] There was a hill on the edge of town that was his sacred place. He wasn't a religious man in that he didn't put much spiritual value on the religious traditions of his people, the sacrifices and endless set of rules and expectations. Not that he was a rule breaker, just that he considered all the rules to be products of a different age. He wondered what the great What Is really thought about if folks did any work on Saturday or not. He wasn't much of a philosophical sort either. He didn't even know how to read. His brother, Andy, had gotten him curious about some of what our resident self-proclaimed prophet Ian was on about, prophecies and philosophies and speculations about what changes must come in the world and that it was all about to change soon. Simon was practical. To go fishing meant to catch fish. To make pottery meant to see the end result of finished pots sitting on the shelf in the store. To spiritually awaken meant to experience a change in heart, an awakening, a direct-connection to What Is. That is what he was searching for on his long walks in the hills. Any philosophical speculation, any prophetic has-to-bes, any extracted from sacred scripture insights, would have to have meaning in the immediate and directly experienced fish nets and clay pots of life.

This brings up a couple of brothers that Andy and Simon knew from the fishing business, Jake and Ian.[9] They were brothers, but different as light and sound. As they say, still waters run deep, and their mindsets were not typical of fishermen. Or perhaps because they lived such a lifestyle that trying to have it all make sense came with long hours of sitting on a boat and waiting for life to happen. Jake was a black and white sort of man, good and evil, trues and falses, rights and wrongs. A very religious man, well respected, he looked the part, he

---

[8] Matthew 14:23

[9] Mark 1:19 Jake is Iakobos, James. Ian is Ioannes, John.

walked the walk. He had no visible vices, no known skeletons in his closet, nothing to be disrespected for. He spoke intelligently, as a man educated, as a man with a passion for accumulating and sorting out the collection of truths that he had inherited from his spiritual tradition. It went back centuries, thousands of years, and it stood for what was timeless, what transcended cultures and ages and peoples. He was carrying the torch, playing his part in the grand scheme of things. For those who shared the same vision, played along to the same expectations, avoided the prescribed vices to be avoided, limited themselves to conversations about approved topics and agreed upon conclusions, it was a safe world of known boundaries and expectations. Play along and prosper within this system. Jake played the game well. He was looked up to as a leader, as a point of contact, as a representative of the tradition. In other circumstances, Jake would have been a priest, and he really thought of himself in that light, but in the reality of the day at hand he was a fisherman. His father ran a boat that docked in the village of Nahum, just a stone's throw away from Bethsaida where Andy and Simon maintained their father's boat. Jake and his brother Ian were friends with Andy and Simon, getting together to exchange fishing tales, exaggerating the quantities caught and the intensity of the storms endured.

Ian was a philosopher. He wanted all the answers to all the questions that folks like Jake dared not even ponder. He expanded his set of inspirations to include anything and everything he could get his ears next to. He explored different opinions, varying perspectives, alternative paths, with a driving quest to find an underlying set of truths. He excluded no one in his quest, no far-fetched doctrine, no obscure dogmatic assertion. He collected thoughts and wove them back together in the fabric of a reality he was weaving just for himself. Risen in his own world of thoughts, his life became a wilderness of solitude. Who could he discuss his insights with? No one would understand. With his collection of answers to which he had yet to find the questions, he stumbled through life as a prophet of what he wanted to call truth, but it seemed somehow incomplete and unsatisfying. He bounced back and forth between the bliss of aha moments and the gloom of the solitude of having no one to share them with. His idealism met the crossroads of having to immerse himself in the fishing business. He would sit and contemplate the meaning of it all while mending the nets for the next day's voyage.

Simon was a bit of a self-induced outcast free spirit wandering misfit. He didn't have the rabbi connections of his friend Jake, but for some reason the religious game of show was not for him anyway. Never mind that he didn't have the credentials to even have a valid opinion in that crowd. Couldn't write his Curriculum Vitae, unless a blank page would suffice. He neither had the patience nor time to explore every religious tradition on the planet like his friend Ian. He collected a few choice quotes that inspired him here and there, but all in all it was way too much work to learn what everyone thinks and then analyze his weighted and well considered opinion of what was smart and what was rubbish, who was on the trail to something real and who was off on a dead end mind game. This self-admitted spiritual blindness, this agnosticism, could be seen as a hamper to Simon's background longing quest of understanding how it all fits. But Simon didn't want to just learn a set of thoughts to repeat them back like a trained parrot. He didn't want to just have to agree to absurdities and go through the motions and hope it all makes sense in the end. He was just hoping if he sat down beside the lake and was quiet enough and focused enough that the wind would whisper the Secret to him. He was just childish enough to dream that one day he'd pick up a rock and hold it in his hand and everything would become crystal clear. He would kick over a stick with his foot and it would be like one of those aha moments that the philosophers describe, where it all makes sense without having to learn or prepare or actually do anything to provoke it. He had this lingering nudge that his life was a dream and that he was one small shake from waking up. What would it be like to be awakened from this dream? He had nothing to offer. If he saved up and make a big donation to the religious institution, what would that gain him? A gold star on the wall? If he saved up and paid to attend school to learn the philosophies of the world, what would that gain him? He was poor in the sense of not knowing how to save up and acquire That Which cannot be bought. It seemed to him that if it could be bought it was somehow not eternally worth anything. What was the currency of eternity? He didn't know but he was certain it didn't have a picture of Caesar on it.

Jude was Simon's only son.[10] Jude represented him to the young world out there. He was the kid that was visible to the village, the one always running down the street, with his life in his hands, a pouch of money on his belt[11], big dreams and ambitions about how to make it in a world that revolved around tangible values. He could see the big picture, had big intentions, with the talk and walk and connections to back up the fate of his taking over the whole world, at least in his own mind. He didn't want to get away from it all. He wanted to control it all. His contacts were with the powerful and influential in the circles that mattered. He knew how to manipulate them into thinking they wanted just what he had to offer. From his fancy red ink to the imported Egyptian paper, and personalized pottery, he had a stream of loyal customers from the well-to-do crowd from Jerusalem.

Martha was Simon's wife. A practical girl, she ran the household with an organization and efficiency that had to be admired, forever knowing her place, always being just what was expected of a young Jewish girl. She took care of her sick mother along with her husband Simon. She inherited the family business from her mother, Mary. Joseph, her father, had died. He was a lot older than her mother and she barely remembered him. When she married Simon, they took over the business and brought new life into the old pottery store.[12] Now that they were both a bit older, their son, Jude, was the face of the business for the

---

[10] John 6:71

[11] John 13:29

[12] Matthew 26:6 The Aramaic for leper (geraba) was confused with the Aramaic for potter (geriba).

village. On a high shelf was a row of drinking cups made by Mary years ago. She was obsessed with intricate patterns and symmetrical form. It was obvious which ones were hers. She hadn't made any in years, since she became sick. Even after she got better, she hadn't gone back to making pottery. Mary's work was gathering dust. Anyways, Martha didn't really want to part with her mother's "art" as she called it. Martha's work was more practical and utilitarian, at least in her own assessment.[13] Martha didn't know what to think about her mother. Martha considered herself more practical, down to earth, with a good head. Mary was a flighty free spirit, Martha concluded, an exotic colorful bird in a world of pigeons. Martha often wondered what it would be like to just let go, but there is so much stuff that just has to get done. The pottery won't make itself, she reasoned. She was right, I suppose. But in the long run there are more important things than having a bowl to eat from or a cup to drink from. Getting close to suppertime, that opinion might change. Perhaps Martha was there on some sort of divine purpose to supply a sense of balance and realism to the mixture of Mary and Simon.

What more can be said about Simon's live-in mother-in-law? She was indeed a strange misfit of a gypsy character, marching to the beat of a drummer that the locals had obviously never heard of. She had a mysterious past and because she was different, the villagers began all sorts of rumors about her. She carried with her a secret tradition, the sort that can get you on the wrong end of a witch-hunt if you happen to live in the wrong place and time. She was living with them, sick and aging, mostly confined to bed. Apart from her daughter and Simon, for this period of her life she never spoke to people anymore. In her younger days she tried, but most never stopped to listen, distracted by their busy lives. Simon was often drawn to the dreamland curiosity of Mary, but she was getting old and the passion was fading into frequent naps and the eclectic was being swallowed by the mundane.

Andy was Simon's brother, still worked on the fishing boat that belonged to their father. Simon grew up on that boat, but after getting married had been spending most of his time in the shop. He learned pottery and how to negotiate buys and sells and interface with the public in the marketplace system of giving each and every thing a value. It was a world system of putting a price on everything and everyone. Even abstract concepts such as skill and time were given a price. Quality workmanship would grant a simple man a fairly good life when the wealthy came to purchase practical and frivolous dust collectors. As Jude had grown up, he let him deal more so with the money dealings. It seemed somehow satisfying, and yet empty at the same time. Even going back to Andy and the endless task of scooping fish out of the lake with nets seemed somehow eternally pointless. Wine in a self-crafted drinking cup and a piece of broiled fish from Andy's net stared up at Simon as dust in the air

---

[13] Luke 10:40

glistened in the daylight coming through the window. This is my blood,[14] Simon laughed as he sipped from the cup he'd made, my life's work. As he pulled the bones away from the piece of fish he placed in his mouth, the thought came to mind, this is my body.[15] I am like this fish, swimming through life, fat dumb and happy, until one day the big net in the sky comes for me. Laughing, he finishes the last of the wine in his cup. Andy's vision was simpler, give him a clear day and a freshly mended net, and fate would take care of supplying him with the fish. His world was small, but very sharp and focused. He was a secret fan of Ian's philosophical ramblings, and he wanted Simon to get enthused about some different grand answer to it all every few weeks at a time. Then just as quickly he would be on about the next great realization secret that could change the way that everyone thought about everything. It was all good fun to him, because none of it really hit home once the nets were mended and the fish were being reeled in. Simon humored Andy, and secretly thought some of the ideas from Ian were pretty clever. It was one of those winds blowing from a strange way sort of days where the stars lined up or something. Andy came in excited about Ian's latest craze of the month. This one was different, he said. What if God was one of us? What if we could reach out and touch What Is directly? Jesus. The name just echoed in the ears of Simon like a ringing sound after hearing a loud explosion. What made this report from Andy any different from the rest? You have to come and experience it for yourself, my brother. You can do a lot with Jesus, Andy explained, a little goes a long way. I saw him by the fire when I was eating fish.[16] I can still feel the result of having had that experience. It is awesome, I tell you.

Jesus was one of those concepts that propels you into the next higher orbit. Jesus stood there in this special dimension that could not be contained and defined and controlled by Jake, nor could it be understood and rationalized and integrated with any sense of organized philosophical thought by Ian. It was a direct-connect to where you could see into What Is in a way that could never be contained nor explained. It was beyond structures of religious institution, beyond ritual, beyond sacred texts, beyond tradition. It was beyond rational scientific explanation of how you can just know something out of the blue, how you can just intuitively know That Which cannot be explained or even defined, much less understood in any sense of logical thought process. Jesus was this vision burning a light into the darkness of the mind, a light clearer than the highest definition most detailed patterned picture you could imagine. Jesus didn't live in some holy building with locked doors, well, not any more so

---

[14] Mark 14:24

[15] Mark 14:22

[16] John 21:9-10

than in some abandoned lot on the edge of town. Jesus supplied direct-connect inspiration of words and ideas that were immediately more meaningful and relevant and practical than anything that could be scraped out of even the most inspired of the collection of sacred texts. Jesus spoke to each in the language they could understand, at the level they were at, at the direction they needed to be going in at the time. The dead zombies of mindlessly following rituals and reciting words and agreeing to believe in the most incredulous absurdities could catch a whiff of Jesus and actually come back to life for the first time since they were small children. There are none too poor, none too stupid, none too immersed in bad habits, none too far gone away from the Light to fail to notice when Jesus shines in their hearts. Simon knew he was onto something big, something that would shake the worlds of his friends, something that would change his very life. It was so simple and yet so complicated. Jesus didn't fit in well with Jake's literalist mindset perfectionism through identifying and obeying all of the rules of life game. Not to say that the Jesus experience excluded playing by the rules. It just made it a bit silly and childish and meaningless. And Jesus didn't fit in well with Ian's philosophical quest to make sense of it all. Jesus was experience than meant more than faith, more than logic, more than having it all make sense.

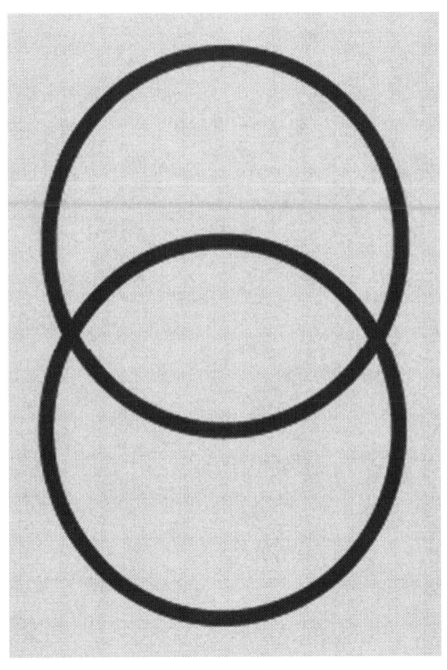

Jesus Gnosis 10

Boat related events

It was one of those surreal moment events[17], on that dreamland border between real and imagined, between experienced and missed. Andy and Simon were in the village of Nahum visiting Jake and Ian. They had just finished helping them mend their nets. Sitting on the docked boat they watched the stars come out on the clear night. The sea was calm. Suddenly out of nowhere a storm blew in, rain and wind, rocking the boat, uncalming the sea. The boat left the dock as if untied by the storm and they found themselves so far out they could not see the shore. Up and down the boat bounced and they all panicked and grabbed oars and tried futily to gain some semblance of control over the situation. Then there on the water appeared a mysterious light, like a campfire glowing, well if it wasn't in the middle of a lake that is. The light inched closer. Andy stared out past the streams of rainwater running down his face and shouted, it is Jesus! What? It is Jesus, Andy repeated. Ian responded in his control freak way that he no longer thought about Jesus, that he had moved on to look for another answer,[18] one that could make the blind see and the lame walk and lepers cleansed and deaf hear and dead raised, just like he read in his studies.[19] This Jesus in his observation had thus far accomplished none of these things. A few coincidences of sick folks recovering and unbelievable tales of turning water into wine does not make this Jesus the be all and end all of his philosophic quest for the Answer. He looked out over the storm drenched waters and could see nothing. Jake saw what Andy was on about and reacted, it is a ghost! With all of his believed-in traditions of burning bushes and talking snakes and Noah's ark and Jonah in a whale, all of the supernatural stuff was relegated to the distant and safe past, and most definitely not to the immediately expressed and directly experienced tonight. As the apparition drew closer, the details of Jesus became apparent, except perhaps for Ian who was busy looking the other direction and beating the waves with a couple of oars. It is Jesus, Andy insisted again. Simon agreed. What was Jesus doing walking on the water and visiting them in a storm? What did he want from them? If it is you, Jesus, Simon shouted out, tell me to walk out on the water and come to where you are. Come on, Simon, Jesus said without saying a word but with the meaning immediately understood by Simon at least, and perhaps by everyone present. Simon stood by the edge of the boat on the side by the light and jumped into the water. For a moment he stood on top of the water face to face with Jesus and a connection was being made, one of those connections that lasts a lifetime, maybe more. In a moment of reality sinking back in to his bliss, Simon had the fleeting thought that he could

---

[17] John 6:16-21 , Mark 6:45-52

[18] Matthew 11:2-3

[19] Matthew 11:4-6

not actually be standing on top of water, that it wasn't possible, that all this must be some sort of dream.[20] Immediately everything changed. The storm stopped. The sky cleared and it was morning. The boat was tied to the shore and Andy and Jake and Ian were asleep on the deck. Simon was standing in the water beside the boat. What was this vision he had? What did it mean? What did it want from him? How could he explain his Jesus to the others? He had to get back home and discuss this with Mary.

Mary sat with her eternal sense of wisdom that transcended anything that modern people could manage to record and recite and carry around with them. She smiled as Simon told her his story about Jesus walking on the water in the storm. I experienced that too, years ago, when I was very young, Mary offered. The meaning is symbolic, as is the meaning of all dreams. Like Joseph of old[21], we must look beyond the literal details of the dreams to uncover the deeper intention of what is trying to be explained to us. Explained? By who, Simon asked. Maybe the "what" will lead to the "who", Mary answered. The boat is life. The people in the boat are the various ways of thinking about and dealing with life. The storm represents the trials and difficulties of life. But in all of the rain hitting you in the face and the wind blowing against you, there is a constant, a light that is as distant or close as your consciousness will admit it to be. It can be anywhere from completely unreal to up close and empowering of miracles. You did actually walk on water, didn't you? For a moment, but yes, and it was beyond description. The water is your normal way of thinking, the flows of habitual thoughts and reactions, learned expectations and prejudices. To rise above the water, to walk on the water, to be immersed in the light that allows you to stand above the water is symbolic of evolving your spiritual state to something above and beyond the normal mundane way of thinking. Born again of the wind that is above the water, what do you think you should do with this new life? Not everyone has this opportunity, or at least, not everyone is open enough to accept and react to such an opportunity. Take hold of it. To those who have a little, more shall be given. To those who can't grab the opportunities that do come, fewer and fewer revelations will come.[22] Jesus is more real than anything out there, but, to those who don't have the eyes to see and the ears to hear, he doesn't exist. You've been my rock, dear Simon, since you've come to my house. You revived me with hope. Not many people have known Jesus, but upon the rock of your faith I could see a community of

---

[20] Matthew 14:22-33

[21] Genesis 40:8-9

[22] Mark 4:24

believers one day form.[23] Keep your eyes open and your ears alert. Jesus has great things in mind for you.

What was it about Mary that opened up the connection to Jesus to such a degree? Why her of all people? She wasn't even religious from a study the scriptures and learn all the rules definition. She wasn't even a philosopher. She just had this appreciation for the simple things of life, the flowers in the field, the birds flying in the sky, dancing to music, good wine, sunsets. Mary described herself as different in the same way as turning on a light is different from being in the dark. She found a way to turn on the spiritual light from within which everything looks differently.[24] It was this light that made her to see Jesus, or perhaps rather, this light was Jesus. He was the secret Answer in a world run by ignorance and inept confusion. A Truth beyond silly rules and dividing line fears of differences, Jesus was a real force within Mary that was stronger than the artificial structures of religious foundations offered by the dull and gullible out there. If you just take an animal to Jerusalem and have them kill the poor thing, you are supposed to be alright with God. If you want to know what God has to say to you, it is what had been written centuries ago and it will have to be properly interpreted by those specially trained to do so. And as long as you don't do any work on Saturday, never eat bacon, wash with a ritual sense of purity, and only associate with "decent folk" then you can wear the label of being a good Jew. All these things seemed so shallow to Mary, so missing some bigger Point that was just below the surface, ever present and yet missed by most everyone. I don't think Jesus had to cast these demons out of her mind,[25] she was strong willed and they were already dying before she ever thought of Jesus. Jesus just gave a seal of authenticity to her eclectic mindset, as if to say that she wasn't the crazy one because she was different. They were the crazy ones because they couldn't see what Mary could see.

A convert to our way of thinking, Nathan, was also a fisherman. He wanted to have a Jesus experience, so he invited us all out on his boat.[26] Simon arrived with his son and mother-in-law. His son tagged along because he was curious about what Simon and Mary were on about. He wanted to reach out and touch this Jesus or sit back and laugh in their faces.[27]

---

[23] Matthew 16:17-18

[24] Mark 4:21

[25] Mark 16:9

[26] John 21:1-14

[27] John 20:24-25

Mary went because she felt something was about to happen. She could predict things like that. Anyways, she wanted to get out of the house. Jake and Ian were there, of course. With me along for the ride, that made exactly 7 of us. 7 is one of those numbers that keeps repeating itself in spiritual thoughts. It is somehow lacking, somehow waiting for the 8th to come along and complete it. Ian had been thinking a lot about numbers in the recent days. He had taken up the study of Pythagoras after a wandering holy man came through the area named Apollonius of Tyana.

153 is one of those numbers that has a meaning jump out, well, at least for anyone who's ever studied Pythagoras. If you draw two circles the exact same size and overlap them to where the edge of each circle touches the exact center of the other circle, a pattern of a fish appears, a pattern called Vesica Piscis. The shape of this fish was as if you took measurements of its length and width and for it being 265 long it was exactly 153 wide. So the number 153 carried with it the thoughts of fish and two colliding circles and Pythagorean philosophy. What were the two circles that collided? Two dimensions? Two realities? If our normal reality was one of the circles, what was the other one? If the body, or outside, of each, touches the heart, or middle, of the other, what other dimensional heart can we reach out and touch? What other dimension reaches out and touches our heart? Another way of looking at the symbol is if you drew a cross that was 265 anythings tall and 153 wide, then drew a circle that touched the top and right and bottom ends of the cross, then drew a circle that touched the top and left and bottom ends of the cross, you will have the Vesica Piscis symbol.

Now Jesus has a way of connecting to different people in different ways. There we sat a little out from shore, with our net cast out on the side of the boat away from the shore, and we caught nothing. It was an odd sort of nothing, not just an "only a few" exception to our usual success. There were zero fish in the net. Then I saw a mysterious light appearing on the shore. Mary immediately stood up and faced the light with a focus of her past experience and complete awareness in the flying moment of what was currently being experienced. It is the Lord, she explained.[28] We all understood that she meant it was Jesus. For some reason, the mind plays tricks on you in these situations. I could imagine a circle going outward from us into the water and a circle going out from Jesus on the shore coming out into the water and overlapping in the middle. Mary then said, he wants us to fish on the other side of the boat, meaning toward the shore in the overlapping in the middle zone. Simon gave her that look, the one he reserves for the times when Mary wants him to do something out of the ordinary and when he does it somehow all works out to be some amazing event. They pull up the empty net and throw it in the water on the side of the boat next to the shore. It immediately filled up with fish. It was so full the net almost broke in pulling the fish back in the boat.

---

[28] John 21:7

Simon jumped out of the boat, expecting to walk on the water, but he ended up swimming toward the shore, toward Jesus. When he walked up on the shore, he was wearing this glowing white robe. He wasn't wearing that when he was in the boat. Strange. When we all got to shore there was a little campfire burning. That much light could not have come from just a fire. We sat about the work of dealing with all of the fish just caught. Little Jude, Simon's son, in the way he is obsessed with numbers, has managed to count all of the fish and informed us that there were 153 of them. It was an all time record. 153?[29] Ian perked up in hearing that number, that Pythagorean concept having to do with fish and interpenetrating circles and change through synthesis. It was only what he had been on about for the past few months. Maybe that was the way the Jesus wanted to get through to him in using his numeric symbol to teach about transformation. As long as we are casting out nets away from Jesus, we get nothing, but when we turn to cast our nets toward Jesus, we are completed. It was after this and because of this that we began to draw the Vesica Piscis symbol as an indication of who was in as far as the knowing about Jesus was concerned. Simon hung the symbol over the pottery shop door. Most people just thought it meant that Simon was also a fisherman. Those of us who knew considered it to be symbolic of Jesus having connected us to a greater purpose.

Ian knew there was something to the Jesus stuff. If only he could keep it secret, or at least controlled, and learn how to tap into it, to channel it. He was concerned when he heard that people he didn't know were also talking about Jesus.[30] And he had his hesitations. What about the new talk of Seth? Was Jesus just a passing fad like all the rest? The miracles could be explained as weird coincidences. The signs could just be imagined, read into the situations, like the 153 fish. Where were the blind who could see again, the lame that could walk again?[31] He wanted evidence, proof that this Jesus was the real deal and not just a product of mass hysteria. Was he really the one, the be all and end all, the Answer? Or should he keep looking, keep listening, keep searching?[32] We all have our standards, our expectations, by which we measure things, our box to put things into. I think that there comes a time when you need to drop all that and see things for what they are, as they are, outside of that box. It is like the elements, earth and water, wind and fire. Ian definitely wasn't stuck in the mud, he was indeed swimming in the seas of philosophies and ideas. There comes a time when you need to come up out of the water and into the wind. From the

---

[29] John 21:11

[30] Luke 9:49

[31] Luke 7:22

[32] Matthew 11:3

wind's perspective you can feel the fire of the sunlight. Down under the water you can make out that there is light, but you remain cold and indifferent. Ian was immersed in the water, the sea of his thoughts and understandings. Jesus was something that required you to be immersed in wind, warmed by the fire, reborn to a life that can walk above the water. That was how Simon understood it, and I think he was onto something really big here.

You know when you can't read, all the words look the same. When what you are looking for is trapped in the words, then if you can't read then you are blind to your Answer. When there are secret rooms in forbidden temples, partitioned off holy of holies, then if you are an ordinary person, you are blocked off, you are lame, you cannot reach it. When the expectation is perfection, you find yourself to be a leper. When there are secret societies of philosophic thinkers that keep it all to themselves, you find yourself deaf, unable to hear, unable to connect, unable to get to the Answer. That is, if they really have the Answer. So many secret mystery initiations promise that if you just join up with them that they will eventually give you the Answer. But do they really truly know? If you do this and say that, eat this and drink that, believe this and stand for that, does this initiation really give you the Answer? How much will you have to tithe to them to find out? How many times will they ask for payment before the Secret is revealed to you? That is what made Jesus different. He would appear and turn the wrong into the right, make sense of the storms of life, supply us with purpose and direction.

It was another fishing trip.[33] Andy and Simon were on the boat that belonged to the father of Jake and Ian. It started out as just another typical routine voyage to find the catch of the day. They were at the same place that the catch of 153 fish had taken place. They went to that same spot often, hoping for, expecting, another miracle, another sign. Simon was sleeping. A storm came out of nowhere, one of those that goes from blue skies to heavy rain without warning. Jake and Ian and Andy were panicking. Water was filling the boat, and they were bailing it out. The wind rocked the boat and they were afraid it was going to capsize. Simon was dreaming of a blissful faraway place, unaware that the rain was striking his back as he slept. Wake up, Simon, Andy screamed. Don't you care? We are going to sink. This is a really bad storm. Simon opened his eyes as if transfixed by a vision. Jesus, he called out. Then as quickly as the storm had appeared, it was gone. A quiet calm surrounded the boat, blue returned to the sky, the sounds of birds flying by the shored meant that the storm was over. They looked at the nets and they were once again full of fish. Simon stared up at the warming sun, causing the water to evaporate on the deck of the boat. He was in another place. Jake and Ian and Andy did all of the fishing work without him. Simon was fishing in another dimension now.

---

[33] Mark 4:36-41

Wanderings of Simon

When Jesus appeared to Mary, she sat up in bed for the first time in months. It was as if an old friend had finally returned. She hadn't felt this way since Joseph had died. It was as if now that Simon had come that a void was filled in her life, a filling that was a requirement for Jesus to once again appear before her. Simon was the son she never had, one to carry on the torch that she could not seem to pass to Martha. She could see that spark of childlike wonder in Simon that could reach out and touch the unreal and transfigure it into something tangible and meaningful. It was at the moment at which Simon "found Jesus" that she began to feel better. The two events had to be related. It was also at this same time that Jude was born, the child of Simon and Martha. Now Jude was to be Simon's undoing, but perhaps in a way he needed to be undone.

Jude never could see Jesus, well at least back then. These days he is perhaps the greatest missionary teacher of the entire movement. Back then was different. All he knew was his father and grandmother had gone nuts and they were spilling expensive oil all over the floor with glazed over looks in their eyes.[34] What are you doing? Why are you wasting that? That is expensive stuff. It was from the shop where the family sold handcrafted pottery and specialty items such as the fancy red ink that they used to emphasize that certain words were especially the words of God. This particular jar contained oil that was customized to be used for religious initiation rituals to indicate that the philosophies had all been learned, the rituals correctly performed, the dos done and the don'ts never done. It was confirmation of a rite of passage. Why this waste? Why cut into the bottom line profit margin for the family business just because grandma got strong enough to get out of bed? Something had to be done. He didn't even know his father anymore.

Yes, the betrayal. I think every story of anyone advancing and accomplishing anything out of the ordinary and meaningful has to include someone in the mix that is pushing against the hero. Reality imitates fiction in this regard. The source of the opposition is what came as such a shock. You couldn't see it coming if you had your eyes wide open and your ears tweaked to hear every whisper. Jude had them come for Simon to take him away to "some place safe" for him. He's out of his mind, you know.[35] The man I kiss is my father; take him away.[36] You will be paid well if you just take care of him and keep him safe.

---

[34] Mark 14:4

[35] Mark 3:21

[36] Mark 14:44

The doors were open when Simon woke up[37], he walked out into the sunlight. I don't think it quite yet registered that Jude had betrayed him, lost faith in him, turned him over to strangers. He wandered around like he didn't remember his own life with Martha and Jude and Mary. As a man possessed by his driving passion, he set out walking seemingly aimlessly, but not all that wander are lost. He lay down in an empty field underneath the stars. Awakened just before dawn, he opened his eyes to see the Morning Star[38] just above the horizon. A voice echoed in his head, I am the bright Morning Star. Simon understood that voice to be that of his Jesus.

Where would he have to go to be understood enough to share his visions? Would the mystics on the mountain in Samaria understand? Would the religious experts in Jerusalem understand? His own wife and child didn't get him. His friends were curious, but not fully with him when it came to his Jesus experiences. Was there anyone out there anywhere on the entire planet that has had the same experiences?

Simon wandered into Samaria, and reached the famous place where ole Israel himself drew water from a well. It was a little wide spot on the trail called Sychar. The Samaritans held the belief that they preserved a purer tradition and that the Jerusalem Temple crowd had taken something real and powerful and had reduced it to what it had become. Simon stopped because he was thirsty and went up to a well. A woman was there getting water. Say, could you get me some of that water, I'm really tired and thirsty? She looked up, aren't you Jewish? I never heard of a Jew taking to a Samaritan in a friendly sort of way. Simon saw Jesus standing there. He explained to the woman, if you could only see the Gift from God, you could be drinking water than never runs out, an inner fountain that springs eternal.[39] Simon could see that he wasn't getting through to her and she wasn't giving him any water. Go and bring back your husband, Simon asked. I don't have a husband, she answered. Jesus shows six men beside her, five to her right and one to her left. Simon replies, ah yes, you have had five husbands and the man you are with now is your future husband. She answered, you must be a prophet. She took this as an opportunity to ask a question that was on her mind for some time. Samaritans worship on the mountain while Jews worship in Jerusalem, so who is doing it right? Simon saw Jesus spread out his arms as if to embrace the whole world. Simon was inspired to answer, the time has come when true worshippers find the Spiritual Father and connected to in a spiritual way.[40] This means that it doesn't matter where you happen to

---

[37] Acts 5:19

[38] Revelation 2:28

[39] John 4:10

[40] John 4:23

be. And you don't need to bring an animal to be sacrificed. The Spiritual Father is beyond such things. She sat down her water jar and ran away into the village. Simon at last got to have his drink.

What did it mean to sit in the very place where Israel stood with his son Joseph all those many centuries ago? Simon sat refreshed with the sacred water of the Samaritans and it got dark. He looked up at a clear night sky and could see more stars than he had ever been able to see looking up at night from the town of Bethsaida. It was a nice night out and Simon slept beside Jacob's well.

Simon got up and began walking before dawn on a vision quest that forced him to the top of the mountain on the edge of the town where Jacob's well was located. To Simon it was the mountain peak from which Moses had received the gift of the Law from the burning bush,[41] where Elijah had received the gift of Prophecy from the still small voice.[42] He could see himself there in a detached dreamlike state, and he looked like the Jesus that he loved. He could see Jake there, morphed into Moses. How he knew he now looked like Moses was unknown. But in his mind Jake was now Moses. Ian appeared, and he transformed into Elijah. Three ways converged on the mountain peak. Could the three commingle? Could the rigidness of Law and the agreed upon prophecies of the philosophers live in harmony with the Direct-connect of his Jesus? What if he built a three-part monument, honoring each tradition?[43] What if he added his Jesus as a "new testament" to append to the Law and Prophets? The idea seems plausible. Then it hit. One of those zappings-from-beyond moments of insight. Jesus was the Direct-connect, the Voice of the Beyond, the Channel for understanding what the Law could not dictate and the Prophets could not foresee. Daylight came and Jake was no longer there. Ian was no longer there. He had stopped imagining them, stopped incorporating them into his new mindset. Only Jesus remained.[44] Only Simon remained. This experience was a turning point in the life of Simon to say the least. Simon thought about what made Jesus different. Both Jake and Ian were carrying on traditions left behind by flesh and blood people. They may have been good people, smart people, even connected to something real people, but they were just people passing on people ideas or some interpretation thereof. Jesus was a "Father in heaven" direct-connection. Perhaps others in the past had had such a direct-connection and that is what some of the Law and

---

[41] Exodus 24:12-18

[42] 1 Kings 19:8-15

[43] Apocalypse of Peter 16:1-13 , Mark 9:5-6

[44] Mark 9:8

Prophets and Philosophers were talking about. But wouldn't it make sense if you could direct-connect yourself to get it straight from the horse's mouth, as Philip would say, that your own personal Holy Spirit experience was more important and real than what you could interpret from writings that were by now centuries old?

Simon was reported to be missing from the home that Jude had arranged for him. Jude is by now very sorry for turning him in and letting them take him away. Mary goes to the place they were holding Simon and sees the opened door. Simon was gone. Where was he? He didn't come back home, and who could blame him.

Sometimes you can't begin a new adventure until you complete and wrap up your current adventure. You can't ride the next horse until you get off of the one you are riding now.[45] You can't try out the new bow for shooting arrows unless you put down the old bow you are holding. Life is like that. Simon knew that he was being summoned to a purpose that was more than fishing for fish or forming pottery. He had to share Jesus with those who could appreciate the experience. He had to fish for people who could let themselves become caught in the net of his enthusiasm about directly connecting to What Is. He had to form lives who could make a difference in the world. He could make the blind see that they didn't need any of the written words of old to read the face of the day at hand and how God is working as we speak. He could make the lame understand that they didn't need to get into some secret room or exclusive initiation into some forbidden mystery to get to the Answer. They could reach the Answer from wherever they happened to be and with whatever tools that they had in hand. They could pick up a rock and it was holy.[46] They could turn over a fallen tree branch and it was sacred.[47] The deaf can now hear because nothing is whispered about What Is. It is shouted from the rooftops when the flock of birds take off into the sky. The rocks shout it out. The flowers growing on the side of the road sing its song. Simon had to wake up, shake up, the living dead of the world. They have been so conditioned, so frozen in their lack of expectations for something real, something direct and personal, something sacred in their mundane lives. They are not poor, they are rich. Jesus is all around them, at their beckon call. There is no tithe to pay, no ritual of initiation, no secret handshake entrance into some great mystery. Life is the mystery and your membership card is your belly button.

Simon was contemplating how fragile fate could be for any of us. He had been fortunate, adaptive, strong, successful in the fishing business and in the pottery business. There were

---

[45] Thomas 47

[46] Matthew 3:9

[47] Thomas 77

those too sick, outcasts, living on the edges, in the shadows, the lepers of the world. They didn't belong, couldn't belong. Somehow his Jesus seemed to also include them, the leper outcasts, along with other types of people who were not "decent folks" like himself. It was one brushstroke away from potter, geriba in Aramaic, the language we spoke, to leper, geraba in Aramaic. The play on words amused Simon. What if he made himself an outcast, embraced poverty, even homelessness, became a wandering ascetic adventurer, like that Apollonius of Tyana that came through town a year or so before? The birds didn't make pots and they seem to thrive.[48] The flowers don't go fishing and they are doing just fine.[49] Who needs all this stuff? Who needs to keep wearing the face that greets the customers at the door? How many people could be reached in Bethsaida, or even in the village of Nahum? It was time to answer the call, pull out his stake and follow Jesus. The wind blows where it will blow and you hear its sound, but you never know where its been or where it will arrive at next.[50] This is how being born again feels like. Simon was resolved.

Jerusalem seemed to draw him like a magnetic force. Or was it more like a moth being drawn to a flame? It was his first time in the city, and the first time in any place so crowded, so diverse, so what he then thought of as cosmopolitan. He found the Temple grounds and just stood there in utter disbelief of how crassly commercial it was. Money changing crooks fleecing the faithful pilgrims. Boxes of poor little doves slated to be bled to death in the name of religious tradition. Do any of them know Jesus? Any of the duped pilgrims coming to supposedly right themselves with God? Any of the merchants? Any of the actual priests? He saw Jesus appear, the way he appeared on the lake, surrounded by storm and wind and force. He turned the tables over that controlled the money exchange and blew the money around for the people there to scurry for and try to pick up as much as they could. He blew the doors of the cages open and all of the sacrificial victim doves cooed off into the rain soaked sky. Simon could see him there with his golden whip, leaving chaos behind him in the entire vast grounds around the Temple. The thunder seemed to actually speak the words, a house of prayer should not be a den of thieves.[51] Simon knew he was justified in his repulsion to the organized religion nonsense there in Jerusalem. This was not the destination he was looking for.

---

[48] Matthew 6:26

[49] Matthew 6:28

[50] John 3:8

[51] Mark 11:17

It was then that a group of men came toward him with handfuls of large rocks and when they got close enough to him they began throwing the rocks at him. It was his introduction to the representatives of the Jerusalem priesthood. They had seen the damage from the winds that surrounded Simon and had caused the tables to flip over and the birds to escape their cages and the coins with the graven image of Caesar to be spilled out and everybody who was trying to make a profit off of the religious pilgrims was upset. They somehow got in their mind that it was Simon who was responsible, that he was a demon possessed magician that represented a force that was directly opposed to the force that the Temple cult was centered around. They were not wrong. Simon saw Jesus standing there, making the rocks miss hitting Simon. Then Simon felt that he became invisible and saw Jesus motioning for him to walk toward him. That meant walking right into the angry crowd of priests with stones. Simon did as Jesus instructed and it was as if they didn't see him.[52] Jerusalem was most definitely not the destination he was looking for.

> And now send men to Joppa, and call for one Simon, whose surname is Peter: He lodgeth with one Simon a tanner, whose house is by the sea side: he shall tell thee what thou oughtest to do.[53]

Wandering on, Simon came to the ancient city of Jaffa. It was beside the Great Sea. Legend has it that it was built by Japheth the son of Noah after the Flood. It was the port that saw Jonah try to escape his destiny and depart on his voyage to Tarshish.[54] Perhaps this was also Simon's escapism. He was disillusioned by Jerusalem, disenchanted by the very structure and essence of his religion. It was here that Simon stumbled across an opportunity to make writing skins, useful for those who thought they still had something to say. Being a port city, there was a growing trade for skins and papers and inks. One of his customers agreed to a trade, writing skins in exchange for teaching Simon to read and write, as that was something he always wanted to learn how to do. The house he lived in overlooked the Great Sea. It made the little lake beside Bethsaida seem like nothing in comparison. The water went all the way to Rome, and beyond. It put his little world into a larger perspective. It wasn't like Jerusalem. There were ideas and idealistic people coming into port from places far away, from Alexandria, and from Rome, from Ephesus, and occasionally some who had even ventured as far as Briton. But Jaffa wasn't like tapping into the spiritual dimension of Jesus, it

---

[52] John 8:59

[53] Acts 10:5-6

[54] Jonah 1:3 , called Joppa, which is the same as Jaffa.

was down to earth and all too politically real. Perhaps down to earth was the direction Simon needed, at least for now.

More and more the Roman soldiers began coming into the port. They were getting ready for something out of the ordinary. Tension filled the air. The revolutionaries were gaining support. Simon knew this from some of his customers that bought skins to record their war plans. He knew it from the tension he felt in his visit to the Temple grounds in Jerusalem. It didn't take Jesus appearing to let him know that something really bad was just over the horizon of time.

One day, one of the soldiers was really upset, to a frantic degree. He was concerned that his daughter was dying, was already dead, she wasn't moving. As Simon passed where he lived, he could see Jesus by the door, beckoning for him to enter. Simon didn't know the soldier and had not had any dealings with soldiers in his stay in Jaffa. He trusted Jesus enough to walk in and a serene sense of taking charge of the situation overcame him. The soldier and his crying wife stepped aside. Simon could tell he was no ordinary soldier. He was one of the ones in charge, an official, an important man. He could rule his men, control his world, but he was at a loss as to how to help his own daughter. Simon walked over and held one of the little girl's hands and could see Jesus holding the other. Wake up, Simon demanded. The little girl sat up.[55] Give her something to eat, he instructed, and walked out the door.[56] What just happened? It was one of those surreal moments that was to be talked about for years to come. What is life? What is death?

---

[55] Acts 9:40

[56] Mark 5:43

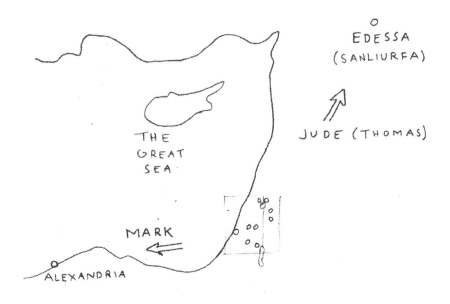

O
EDESSA
(SANLIURFA)

JUDE (THOMAS)

THE
GREAT
SEA

MARK

ALEXANDRIA

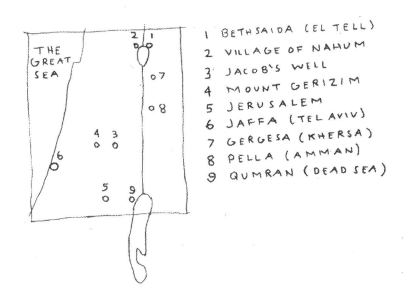

THE
GREAT
SEA

1 BETHSAIDA (EL TELL)
2 VILLAGE OF NAHUM
3 JACOB'S WELL
4 MOUNT GERIZIM
5 JERUSALEM
6 JAFFA (TEL AVIV)
7 GERGESA (KHERSA)
8 PELLA (AMMAN)
9 QUMRAN (DEAD SEA)

Flight to Pella

There was no doubt in his mind that the end was near, the end of peace. It was time to preserve his own, to care about the people back home. Time to warn Martha and Jude, Mary, Andy, Philip, Jake and Ian, Nathan, and anyone else who has ears that can hear. He had heard of a safe place, a city on a hill, above and beyond the chaos of war, out beyond the extant of the Roman Empire, like the way that the gods of the Greeks perch up on Olympus. The time was at hand.

> Those who are exalted above the world are indissoluble, eternal.[57]

What do they hope to gain even if they win their war? Their inheritance of their religious tradition can only give them more of the same that it's been for centuries. Heirs to the dead only inherit death. There will only be more and more of "us against them" and drawing lines and division and fear and hatred. It will never ever end, whether in the guise of full tilt crusades over the promised land or tense cold wars of repressed fears and distrusts. We are heirs to what is Living and our inheritance is life, and not just a being alive because we didn't participate in the war. We will inherit it all. They will inherit nothing. Not only will they not win their war for the control of their tradition of death, they do not even try to win the war to inherit that which is Living. They won't inherit anything. They will be dead. Now we get the best of both worlds. We inherit the Living and we still wake up in their world of dirt and rock. I guess we get the dirt and rock too, since they will be left dead and the Romans will have gone back to Rome. Now we will freely share the Living to be inherited by any of the dead out there who will be willing to partake of it, and it will be theirs forever. They will never have to fight to preserve it, because it can't be conquered.[58]

Mary had been having nightmares. She had visions of a giant red monster with several heads that reached out from snake like necks.[59] The monster was destroying all in its path, knocking down building with its tail, attacking and killing any who stood in the way of any of its faces ripe with sharp fangs and cold calculating eyes. The monster would look directly at Mary with a simultaneous looking from all of its heads at the same time and began lunging toward her. She would wake up at this point, sweating, heart pounding, paralyzed to the bed for a few moments until her wakened state took over and she realized that it was that same dream

---

[57] Philip 53.21-23

[58] Philip 52.6-15

[59] Revelation 12:3

again. She knew it was linked to the war somehow, the Romans, but what did that have to do with a sickly old lady in Bethsaida?

News of the revolution had of course reached Bethsaida already. There was this sense of being forced to support the revolutionaries against Roman occupation in the guise of being patriotic, of being a good Jew, of it being God's will. Mary just had to speak her mind, or perhaps it was the mind of Jesus being channeled through her. Hers was a vision of a world without borders, an extended family of humanity beyond the xenophobia of "us vs. them" mindset. Hers was also a realistic calculated prediction that the Romans would arrive with legion after legion of well-prepared soldiers and kick butt. The Jewish scriptures said a lot about war, about manifest destiny, about promised lands and miraculous defeats of those who would otherwise occupy them. With God on our side, how can we lose? Mary had to speak up. It nauseated her. You know what "the Highest God there is" really wants from us? To show compassion for our enemies.[60] To forgive those who have wronged us.[61] To work for peace in a world of conflict.[62] To embrace diversity.[63] Well, that was a bit too much for some of the patriotic townsfolk to put up with for long. It was confusing the children that they were trying to get into the mindset to prepare for the revolution.

Mary hadn't been in the village for quite some time, what with being bed ridden and with the history she had in Bethsaida of being a "witch" and the thought that she needed to be dealt with by the "decent folk" of town.[64] Fear of the unknown makes lies seem believable and ordinarily easygoing people collectively turn into a monster. As Mary explained it, Jesus had saved her from the clutches of seven demons and freed her, and these seven demons were the very ones playing mind games with most everybody out there.[65] They are so in denial that there is anything wrong with them that they want to point a finger at anyone who can see past the charade of their values and habits and xenophobia. Mary could think outside of their box, live outside of their box, dream outside of their box. In her younger days she had taunted the rabbis, claiming to know God better than them. She associated with foreigners, with those who were "outsiders" to the "good people" crowd. She dared befriend those who

---

[60] Matthew 5:44

[61] Mark 11:25

[62] Matthew 5:39

[63] Matthew 5:45

[64] Exodus 22:18

[65] Luke 8:2

were being shunned.[66] Now while she had been sick, it was a bit of out of sight, out of mind. When Mary emerged and walked through Bethsaida again, it stirred up emotionally charged reactions among a certain rabbi who thought rather highly of himself. There she is, he taunted, that adulterous woman, which was an interesting charge for Mary in that she had only been married once and had been sick and confined to her house since Joseph had died. Well, you know how it goes, enough noise and a crowd gathers, and crowds don't like to think for themselves on an individual basis. They get into this herd mentality where they move and react as if a school of fish. Stone her, stone her, the deranged rabbi shouted. It was just then that Simon returned home for the first time in months. He had just walked into the shop when the situation was getting underway. Simon came running out of the shop to see what was all of the ruckus. A few of the villagers began to pick up rocks, not really knowing what to do next, staring at each other and looking to the rabbi to see what to think and do next. Simon walks up to beside the rabbi, though not completely as himself. He represented, or is it more like channeled, the beloved Jesus of the Mary who was stunned and remembering her disgust for ignorant judgmental fools. As if his hand was being guided by some metaphysical force, Simon began to write in the dirt with a stick. For each man standing around Mary, Simon wrote his name and the worst think he'd ever done. Each in turn dropped their rock and slunk away, hoping no one else had read what they'd done. Some of the brighter ones left before their turn came around. The very rabbi, who had charged Mary with being an adulterous woman, was given the charge of adultery himself when the stick turned to his case.[67] The look on his face was one of those priceless moments that you wish you could have captured as a lasting image. Mary turns to Simon and the two of them are standing there all alone. She realizes that he is back home at last. She runs up to embrace him. Simon hesitates, there is no time for that, we must prepare to depart and to ascend to a safe city on a mountain.[68] Mary walks back inside the store. Simon surveys his hometown as if walking back through it in a dream, the way you do when you visit your childhood home after many years and see how it all changed. Simon had only been gone for a few months, but a lot had changed. Everything looked the same and was laid out the same. It was the talk of revolutionary war, of plots and plans and religious convictions that God would send them whatever help they needed to defeat the Roman Empire. A dark gloomy cloud of impending doom, from Simon's perspective.

---

[66] Mark 2:16

[67] John 8:3-12

[68] John 20:17

Mary swears that he is alive, for she just saw him.[69] Jude said, unless I can reach out and touch him, I won't believe it.[70] He was in repressed denial for having betrayed his father. He thought about how much his father loved him and his only crime was being a bit of a kook. Simon appeared in the house that night and Jude looked at him like he'd seen a ghost. Can I get some fish, I'm hungry, Simon said.[71] Well, ghosts don't eat, Jude thought to himself. He stood up and walked over and hugged his father. I forgive you -- you didn't know what you were doing,[72] Simon said, as he sat down to eat. Martha looked at him with anger and compassion, mad that he'd abandoned her, happy that he was there eating with them once again. After eating, Simon began speaking with a serious tone. We all have to get out of here. We all have to leave. A serious war is coming. Who knows how far it will go, how wide it will spread. Mary nodded. She had been having intuitive insights about this for some time now.

Simon went out to the old boat to find Andy. A meeting was made of Simon's friends, Philip, Nathan, Jake and Ian. Nathan didn't want to leave his fishing business behind. Ian had lost all faith in Simon's obsession with his Jesus encounters and was secretly in support of the war effort, so he didn't want any part in following Simon on a coward's retreat. Ian had a new disciple that became his mentor at the same time, a strange character named Dositheus. Dositheus was obsessed with the legends of Seth, the son of Adam born to replace Abel that had been murdered by Cain. He was proposing to channel this Seth in much the same way that Simon and Mary channeled Jesus. Jake was at one of those turning points, trying to figure out how to reinterpret all of his religious tradition into the modern sense of urgent reality. Did it all end up in one giant fight with the Romans? Did it all end up being opened to a more cosmopolitan set of values, a "Jesus" reinterpretation of what it all was originally supposed to mean? He didn't know. And to make the decision even harder, he was caught between his brother Ian and his friends from Bethsaida. In the end, Jake decided to join the exodus.

I couldn't leave behind that one special horse, the one that Jesus rode, the one that went from unridable and wild to friendly and tame. Mary was too old for such a journey on foot, and so I brought the horse for her to ride. It was as if they were old friends, the horse immediately warming up to her. The rest of the company walked alongside Mary and my horse.

----

[69] John 20:18

[70] John 20:24-25

[71] Luke 24:41-43

[72] Luke 23:34

The destination was Pella, a safe place on the other side of the Jordan from the "promised land" of war and chaos. There they arrived, this small band of "Jesus" people in a world cut off by the upcoming war to the West and the perpetual desert all the way to Edessa in the East.

Gergesa was a city of rich merchants on the edge of the world, the only stopping place on the journey from Bethsaida to Pella. Simon had been there before on a business run to acquire some rare imported writing materials from the East. The tone had changed. Mary felt an empathic sense of dread about the place now, like something really devastating was about to happen there. After the revolution in Jerusalem failed in its Temple shattering Messiah forsaken defeat, it was only a matter of three years until the revolutionaries that barricaded themselves in Masada fell to Caesar Vespasian and his Roman legions of well trained and equipped soldiers. Mary saw a vision of great insanity being driven out of a very dangerous deranged man and infecting a herd of a couple thousand pigs that ran through Gergesa and jumped into the Sea of Galilee and drowned when this powerful man arrived in the town.[73] It was years later that we understood Mary's vision as referring to Vespasian. It was the wildness and insanity that Mary saw in the revolutionary mindset that divided her and the group forever from the Jews that supported the revolution. Even after the conflicts had died down, being Jewish was dangerous. The revolutionaries that managed to run away to Alexandria were dealt with harshly by the Romans. There was no good place to be seen for the time being. Well, almost no place. Pella was an oasis of tranquility in a world gone mad.

Jerusalem was left devastated by the failed revolutionary war. The Temple no longer existed. Not one stone left on top of another one of the massive building.[74] No place for the faithful to come to have animals sacrificed. The end of an era. The great libraries of sacred texts were either destroyed or buried away in jars. Perhaps even in some of the jars Simon had made. Perhaps even written on the skins that Simon had prepared. Perhaps even written using some of the ink that Simon had sold in Mary's store. Perhaps not. But the point was that they were taken out of circulation, out of the relevant context of what was obviously a failed religion from the perspective of the revolutionaries. Simon's Jesus stood the test of time. He could not be knocked down. He could not be ripped apart nor hidden away.

As long as you are in the valley, one of the masses, you look like them, talk like them, think like them, act like them, react like them, you blend in. Once you begin the gnostic ascent, and you reach the view point of your gnostic hill, and you put up the walls to distinguish how

---

[73] Matthew 8:28-32

[74] Matthew 24:2

you think, so that you separate yourself from them, you no longer cherish their blind faiths, you no longer hold their prejudices, you no longer follow their cultural habits, you have reached a point of authenticity, you have built a wall around your own uniqueness. You will be spotted as no longer being one of them, you are in their world but not of their world, you have different values, different goals, different assertions.

The "on a high hill" to me means being up and away from it all. As if a war is going on down there and it is safe up here, which was quite literally the case. You are up and away, you've built a wall around yourself and you are relatively safe from the war of the world out there. This isn't the same as hiding, because you stand out like a sore thumb.[75] Like saying, in the world but not of the world.

> I will make you fruitful and multiply you exceedingly, and kings shall come forth from you, and rule in every place where the sole of human foot shall tread. I shall give to your offspring all the land under heaven, and they shall rule over all the nations as they please. Afterward, they will take all the earth and possess it as an inheritance forever.[76]

Religions inspire. But what do they inspire people to think and do? What hopes and dreams will it give them to justify what they would have to attempt to do to achieve those promises? Nearly all of Judaism was up in arms or supporting the revolution. Why should they be subjugated to the Romans? They should not only throw off Roman rule, they should rule over the Romans, they should rule over everyone that the Romans rule over, they should rule over everyone that the Romans never could defeat and control. The promises were there. The strong shall inherit the earth, the bold and the courageous, those who dare to take a stand and fight against the legions of Roman soldiers. When in doubt they would remind each other that God was on their side and the prophets had promised a great Son of David Messiah king to come to their aid. If these ideas were true and they had strong enough faith and determined enough intention to keep fighting and never lose hope that God will step in and intervene, how could they lose?

The mountain city of Pella was one of those locations that just inspired creativity, demanded something significant come out of the experience. Mount Sinai was the site where Moses was said to have met God, received the Law, and began the religion of Judaism. The Samaritans had their sacred mountain of Gerizim, with legends of Joshua identifying it as the first holy place in Israel after having crossed the Jordan River. To them, this was the origin of the true

---

[75] Thomas 32

[76] Dead Sea Scrolls 4Q223-224 Unit 1.1.1-3 , Jubilees 32:18-19

faith that had been perverted by the Jerusalem Temple cult. Pella just felt like such a monumental place, a site beckoning for being the foundation for the build-up of something big. There was a community of Nazarenes[77] there, a mystical and pure set of spiritually minded Jewish separatists. They wanted nothing to do with the revolutionary war. They considered the rally for violence to be a wicked group mindset insanity that would ultimately fail, leaving them, the weak and the meek, to awaken in the new day of the aftermath of their war, a day that the violent would never live to see.

The Nazarenes were to become the perfect community for Simon and those who followed him. They could see in Simon's "Jesus" that his experiences and mindset and conclusions were like their own. In fact, some of them used the exact same name of "Jesus" to label their metaphysical experiences. In embracing this culture, Simon completed his training in the art of reading and writing. When Jake learned to read and write, it opened up a new world for him. He could now read the scriptures that he had memorized passages out of before. He stood in a very unique position of being the first ever to read the Jewish scriptures with a "Jesus" mindset, at least in the fashion he proceeded to adopt. Another unique thing about his position was that he lived in the one town on the entire planet that was the home of all of the known "Jesus people" that existed at that time. There may have been others, but not as far as we had ever heard of. It was a difficult time to go around exploring and asking questions. These were the planting of the seed days, the tending to the tender young sprout of a new vision for a new age, one that would outlast the war, outlast the Temple, outlast even the Roman Empire. There they sat on the city on the hill that could not be hidden and yet was perfectly safe.[78] They were retreated back across the Jordan, retreated from the promised land, but theirs was a kingdom not of this world,[79] and their king was not one that Caesar could ever defeat with all of his legions of soldiers.

The wise men of Pella already had visions of what was to come in Jerusalem, and even visions of the Jesus that we thought was something unknown outside of our little group. When some of them first encountered Mary, they were surprised. You are the one in my vision,[80] one of them explained, whose name was Mark, I saw your face in the sky, you were dressed with the sun, standing on the moon, wearing a crown of stars. You were giving birth to a child. Another one interrupted, I saw you too, but it was different. I saw a huge red monster with

----

[77] Numbers 6:18-21

[78] Thomas 32

[79] John 18:36

[80] Revelation 12:1-6

many heads that was intent on destroying the child as soon as he was born. O, yes, the Child. I saw him as king ruling as far as could be reached in every direction, but at the same time he was not in this world. He was seated with God. I saw the woman running away, escaping the red monster. She ran to the wilderness, preserved by God, given a safe home. And here you are. You have arrived. Tell us about the Child. Mary explained that she only had the one daughter, Martha, and that she never had a son. How can this be, the wise man from Pella asked her. We saw your stars. We saw the Child. We saw the King that is seated with God. You must be the one, the Mother of our Lord. Mary was speechless. Then one of them took out a drawing, unwrapping the linen cloth that was around it, and showed the picture to Mary. It was Jesus. That sense of heart pounding and can't breathe took over the moment. How did they know her Jesus? How long had the Nazarenes known about her Jesus?

One of the Nazarenes offered a quotation from the Psalms as being especially appropriate on the arrival of Simon and company and their escape from the revolutionary war:

> Behold the eye of the Lord will have pity upon the good ones; and upon those who glorify him will he increase mercies; and from an evil time will he redeem them. Blessed be the Lord who saves **the poor ones** from the hand of strangers; and redeems the innocent ones from the hand of the evil ones;[81]

Mark, the one who had the vision of Mary and baby Jesus, added his own original blessing, which Jake took to heart and remembered:

> Blessed are the **poor** in spirit: for theirs is the **kingdom** of heaven.[82]

Yes, another one added, for Zephaniah of old had foreseen the hiding of the meek:

> Seek ye the LORD, all ye **meek** of the earth, which have wrought his judgment; **seek righteousness, seek meekness**: it may be ye shall be hid in the day of the LORD'S anger.[83]

The first one, who loved to quote the Psalms, offered:

---

[81] Psalm 154:16-18

[82] Matthew 5:3

[83] Zephaniah 2:3

> For evildoers shall be cut off: but **those that wait upon the LORD, they shall inherit the earth**. For yet a little while, and the wicked *shall* not *be*: yea, thou shalt diligently consider his place, and it *shall* not *be*. But **the meek shall inherit the earth**; and shall delight themselves in the abundance of **peace**.[84]

It did not seem like the meek were inherited this world. It was ruled by the ruthless who show no mercy, world leaders that were not very good people by anyone's definition, and the ability to destroy and kill and conquer were the values of the day. Here in Pella it was different. But back in Jerusalem they had not yet learned their lesson. What "earth" shall the meek inherit? Was it a desert wasteland? Was it a world of another dimension? Was it the world from which they had encountered Jesus? Jake considered just what it all must mean, offering to the Nazarene community:

> Blessed are the **merciful**: for they shall obtain mercy. Blessed are the **pure in heart**: for they shall see God. Blessed are the **peacemakers**: for they shall be called the children of God.[85]

Pella was an interesting haven for the "Jesus" people, both Simon's group and the Nazarenes that called it home. It was a refuge from the prevailing Jewish mindset, the Messianic expectations that fueled xenophobia and war. They stood aloof, protected, but open minded to the Jews that wanted to live there. It was a small hidden retreat of a town, but more cosmopolitan in its mindset than any place in Judaea or Galilee or Samaria. Definitely more safe at this point. It became the dreamed of Shangri La of those trapped in Jerusalem by the war. If only they could escape and get to Pella, back across the Jordan, back away from the promised land. But they were trapped, losing their heads, losing their Temple, losing their identity, losing their value, losing their sacred texts, losing their Messianic hopes, losing their self-induced revolutionary war against the Romans. Simon sat looking out at the quiet desert in blissful gratitude that Jesus had pushed him to come to here and to save his family and friends. There was something of greater value at stake then the fighting for the promised land of ancestors long dead. There was a king and a kingdom not of this world to consider.

> Ye are the light of the world. A city that is set on an hill cannot be hid.[86]

---

[84] Psalm 37:9-11 , Matthew 5:5

[85] Matthew 5:7-9

[86] Matthew 5:14

At least at the start of the war, Jews heading away from Jerusalem were considered traitors, unpatriotic, ungodly. The revolutionaries would kill anyone they found trying to desert as a sign to anyone else who wanted to take the cowards way out and so disgrace them and their cause. This is to say that it was fortunate that Bethsaida was so close to the other side of the Jordan, was so convenient for Simon to gather his own and quietly escape from. And fortunate that Simon acted early.

The Nazarenes in Pella had a different way of looking at Jewish tradition than the Jerusalem Jews. They were most definitely not looking for a Messiah hero to drop out of the clouds and assist with a self-induced revolutionary war. They were not looking to rule the world or defeat all of the governments of the world. They were looking for something hidden just beneath the surface of it all, something more real than blind faith in absurd assumptions of what some ancient prophecies really meant. This pacifist resistance seems like a contradiction to their very method of study in itself, which they called pesher. It is where you have one thought in mind and hold that thought and then consider something else and how it relates to that one thought. It was how the Messianic hopefuls had fooled themselves in having blind faith in a winless war. You extract a meaningful significance to here and now from words written centuries ago and far away. You look for the symbolisms, the key words, the threads of ideas woven through, and get back into the mindset in which the texts were written, resurrecting them. For the revolutionaries the overwhelming "one thought" was "Son of David Messiah/Christ" and how the present war was the end of the world for foreign occupation and control and the beginning of a new world in which they ruled. For the Nazarenes, it was the same approach, but a different conclusion. The overwhelming "one thought" was "Jesus" and the texts being mined for the revelations about Jesus were the sacred writings of Jewish tradition. That "Jesus" could be revealed by studying ancient texts was a radical concept unheard of in Jerusalem.[87] They will want to claim it as their idea, but the truth is that they were so obsessed with their own "one thought" of Messiah, of Christ, and how that related to their current experience of revolutionary war, that "Jesus" was nowhere in their mindset. No, for the most part at this time, "Jesus" was limited to Pella, to the Nazarenes and to Simon and his group that were refuges from the war.[88] All of this was a light shining in the darkness to Jake. He could combine treasures old and new, as it were, in maintaining his love for and study of the sacred Jewish texts and relate them to his newfound relationship with Jesus.

---

[87] Acts 17:11 , Acts 18:28 , Romans 15:4 , Romans 16:25-26

[88] Matthew 13:52

> Revelation 21:10 And he carried me away in the spirit to a great and high mountain, and shewed me that great city, the holy Jerusalem, descending out of heaven from God,
>
> Revelation 3:12 Him that overcometh will I make a pillar in the temple of my God, and he shall go no more out: and I will write upon him the name of my God, and the name of the city of my God, which is new Jerusalem, which cometh down out of heaven from my God: and I will write upon him my new name.

There was an overriding thought that permeated the mindset of the Nazarenes at Pella and by infection the minds of Simon and his family and friends. Jake was especially prepared for this, being interested in sacred tradition all of his life.

> **Think not that I am come to destroy the law, or the prophets**: I am not come to destroy, but to fulfill.[89]

Jesus had been all about experience and transformation, direct-connect, channeling something sacred, a magical dimension that reaches down and touches our mundane lives. It was thought by the Nazarenes that this Jesus was known and predicted and even encountered by holy people of old, and thus prophesized about and revealed in the writings of Jewish scripture. If this be the case then it opened up a cosmos of questions. Which of the collected words had meaning? How much can you stretch what something says in the spirit of pesher interpretation? It seemed like some greater hand was guiding the search, leading each seeker to the next aha moment insightful text. Jesus was encountered more so by this study of the texts than by the type of direct experiences that had propelled Mary and Simon thus far. There was before an innocence of not being able to read and thus not being distracted by words. The words were like a tomb in a way, encapsulating and trapping and limiting. Could they preserve Jesus in a way that he could once again come to life in a real sense in the real lives of those who could connect with him? Can logos, preserved words, be a vehicle for, a container for, a transporter for Truth? That had always been the hopes of spiritual writers for centuries.

The prophets reminded Simon of his now lost friend Ian who had gotten enraptured by the war. He knew that the violence he was embracing, the force he was so envisioning, the divine help he had such faith in, would make him lose his head in the end.[90] Whoever carries a

---

[89] Matthew 5:17

[90] Mark 6:24

sword will eventually die from someone else's sword.[91] The eye for an eye mentality was just leaving behind a world of blind people. The blind faith in the coming of the Messiah was destroying everything they had ever stood for and hoped for. The Romans will come dancing across the Great Sea and have Ian's head on a platter. Don't say that Simon didn't warn him and even beg him to come to Pella. Still – sad.

On occasion there were Buddhist monks who had wandered from the East, coming from Edessa, they in the past traveled through Pella to continue a journey to Egypt or Greece. Stopped by the barrier of the war, some of them lingered for a few months before turning around and venturing on back East. In the spirit of doing something to balance out the spirit of violence permeating Judaea and Samaria, they offered the teachings of their Teacher from what sounded like the same place or space as Simon considered Jesus to occupy. Their Jesus was called Siddhartha Gotama. They explained he lived 600 years before and 3000 miles to the East, but his ideas were timeless and transcended cultures and ages. When taken to heart they could transform and awaken. Their ideas, though foreign, were not out of sync with those of the pacifist Nazarenes and the Simon group.

> To anger, respond with peacefulness. To evil, respond with good. To greed, respond with giving. To lies, respond with truth.[92]
>
> Be tolerant with the intolerant. Be patient with the harsh. The holy man shows compassion to all creatures.[93]
>
> You who strike back at one striking you, who scream back at one screaming at you, who plot against the one who plots against you, have already swallowed the bait, already lost control. We do not swallow the bait. We do not lose control.[94]
>
> You who repay an angry man with anger only make things worse for yourself. By not repaying an angry man with anger, you become the victor of a difficult battle.[95]

---

[91] Matthew 26:52

[92] Dhammapada 17:3

[93] Udanavarga 33\:46

[94] Brahmanasamyutta 2

[95] Sakkasamyutta 4

When men beat you and scold you, you must accept it patiently. With hands pressed together bow to them humbly.[96]

Those who take swords and shields and buckle on bows and quivers, charging into battle with arrows and spears flying and swords flashing — they will be found run through with arrows and spears, their heads cut off by swords.[97]

A killer's child becomes a killer. A conqueror's child becomes a conqueror. An abuser's child becomes an abuser. A reviler's child becomes a reviler. The way that karma unfolds, the plunderer will eventually be plundered.[98]

Even if bandits cut you limb from limb with a saw, the arising in the mind of hatred towards them would not be doing as I have taught you.[99]

You should train yourself to remain unaffected of mind, without uttering any evil words, abiding with compassion for the welfare of others, with a mind of loving kindness, with no trace of inner hate. **If anyone should give you a blow with his hand, with a rock, with a stick, or with a knife, you should abandon any revengeful thoughts or words.**[100]

So, what are the rules here, Jake asked. He was in the mindset of collecting a list of dos and don'ts, the letter of the Law, preserved and memorized and followed to the letter. One of the Nazarenes explained that you reach a state of being, a state of connection, a state of channeling What Is to a personal level, that you are in a place beyond the need for rules and regulations. If you have no anger, no intent on revenge, no taking things so personally, then you don't have to be told to not murder anyone around you. You are beyond what that Law would attempt to enforce. If you have no greed, no desire to collect earthly trinkets, no competitive craving to make yourself look rich, then you don't have to be told to not steal from those around you. In fact, you feel like sensing what they need that they don't have and giving it to them. If you are not controlled by lust, by being led around by every passing craving, by loving the simple old fashioned life, then you don't have to be told to not commit

---

[96] Surangama Sutra

[97] Mahadukkhakklandha Sutta 12

[98] Kosalasamyutta 15

[99] Kakacupama Sutta 20

[100] Kakacupama Sutta 6

adultery with the wife of one of those around you. If you value truth beyond all things, you don't have to be commanded not to be a lying witness. You see, the Law becomes of little value for one who embraces the Holy Spirit of What Is. This isn't destroying the Law. This is fulfilling the very purpose and intent of the Law.

> The supremacy of the Kittim shall cease, that wickedness be overcome without a remnant. There shall be no survivors of all the Sons of Darkness. Then the Sons of Righteousness shall shine to all ends of the world, continuing to shine forth until end of the appointed seasons of darkness. Then at the time appointed by God, His great excellence shall shine for all the times of eternity; for peace and blessing, glory and joy, and long life for all Sons of Light.[101]

You are against the revolution then, Andy asked. He was thinking of all that Ian was resolved to fight for and die for. Another one of the Nazarenes spoke up. Theirs is just a temporary revolution, and if they win they will replace one political situation with another, and they may hold control for a few years, but eventually they will fall to something else. They could push the Romans back to Rome for now, but they'll be back. Or some other great movement in the future will roll over them. Kingdoms come and kingdoms go. What we are on about is a Revolution that is lasting and meaningful, transformational, empowering. What results is a kingdom not of this world,[102] a kingdom that Caesar cannot conquer. They are looking to advance the Jews, and just the Jews, the "Sons of Light" against everyone else in the world, which they label as the "Sons of Darkness". Their Messiah is "Son of David", a label for a very small mindset, a very limited group, exclusive, selected, predestined in their way of thinking. I know you are drawn here because you had visions of Jesus. Do you know who Jesus is? He is "Son of Adam", a label for a very broad all-inclusive mindset, including every person on the planet, inclusive, open. Do you see the difference? The "Son of David" Messiah is supposed to meet them in Jerusalem and arrive with angels, come on the clouds of the dust of heavenly warhorses and make sure that the revolution is successful in defeating the Roman occupation. The "Son of Adam" Jesus is also helping with a Revolution that results in the establishment of the New Jerusalem. So, you see, our Revolution is much more important in the long term. And it is for everyone, not just for one limited group of narrow-minded people.

Simon had a vision, what if more people encountered Jesus? How many were there already? Was it just his group and the Nazarenes here in Pella? How far has this Revolution already

---

[101] Dead Sea Scrolls 1QM 1:6-9

[102] John 18:36

extended? Did it mean the same to people in different situations? His vision was to extend Jesus to the world out there, maybe not just yet to the Jews and Romans since they seemed to currently be busy trying to kill each other. But there was Edessa, the home of Abraham, and Ethiopia, and Alexandria in Egypt, and India. Imagine a world united under the same vision and intention and Holy Spirit resolution to bring about the Kingdom of Heaven here on earth, spread around the planet like an unseen presence that connects us all.

The Buddhist missionaries continued to interact and give and take with the Nazarenes. They alternated between listening and teaching, as if they were trying to weave their Buddha into the Jesus mindset. One star filled silent night, they shared the following:

Responding with more hate never defeats hate. Even in this world, hate can be conquered only by compassion. This is the Eternal Law.[103]

We should live with joy and love among those who hate. We should live with joy and health among those who are ill. We should live in joy and peace among those who dwell on conflict.[104]

The enlightened one is full of compassion for all beings. For him there are no transgressions. For him there is no going astray. He is not lost in the confusion, but is wise and ever mindful. For if one does not forgive those who confess transgression, harboring anger, intending judgment, strongly establishing an enmity — this is a very undelightful state to be in. Thus I forgive your transgressions.[105]

There are two types of fools. One does not see a wrong as a wrong. The other does not forgive one who is sorry for a wrong.[106]

He abused me, he struck me, he defeated me, he robbed me — in those who give a home to such feelings hatred will never be conquered. In this world hatred is never conquered by further acts of hate. It is conquered by hating hate itself. This is an Ancient Law carved in stone.[107]

[103] Dhammapada 1:5

[104] Dhammapada 15:1-3

[105] Devatasamyutta 35

[106] Sakkasamyutta 24

[107] Upakkilesa Sutta 6

> Above, below, across — everywhere, to all as to yourself, dwell pervading the entire planet with a mind balanced in love, abundant, exalted, and limitless, with no traces of any hostility or ill will.[108]
>
> With minds remaining unaffected, we should never speak harshly. We should be actively compassionate for the welfare of others. We should possess a mindset of loving-kindness, with no trace of hidden spite. We shall live facing one another with a mind immersed in loving-kindness, and starting with the person next to us, we shall live facing the entire planet with a mind immersed in loving-kindness. In abundance, exalted, without limit, without hostility, without ill will, we should thus train ourselves.[109]
>
> To attain a heart perpetually filled with loving kindness, filled to overflowing, with no room left neither for hatred nor for ill will, this liberating heart of loving-kindness is the way to union with Brahma.[110]

And who is this "Brahma", Simon asked. He is the one you call the "God of Abraham" explained one of the Buddhists. We heard about Abraham in Edessa, how he gave up on the religions of the gods and sought after the ultimate What Is. That is Buddha's quest. To awaken to the direct experience of What Is. He rarely spoke of Brahma, because he didn't want to confuse his followers into thinking in terms of a specific religion about a specific god. To those who understood Brahma, he offered these words. In your context, you could replace Brahma with Jesus and the meaning would be the same. From what we have learned from the Nazarenes here, Jesus of the Nazarenes is loving-kindness, he is having empathy and sympathy for everyone, he is healing and forgiveness and hope. He is active compassion and seeing from a higher perspective than any mundane limited dispute or situation people find themselves in.

How far from this Buddhist and Nazarene way of thinking were the supporters of the revolution? They divided everything into us and them, light and darkness, love and hate, grace and vengeance, assist and kill.

---

[108] Cittasamyutta 7, Vatthupama Sutta 16

[109] Kakacupama Sutta 11

[110] Tevijja Sutta 76-77

Jesus	Messiah / Christ
Ye have heard that it hath been said, Thou shalt love thy neighbour, and hate thine enemy. But I say unto you, Love **your enemies**, *bless them that curse you, do good to them **that** hate you,* and pray for them **which** *despitefully use you, and* **persecute you**;[111]	He is to teach them both to love all the Children of Light—each commensurate with his rightful place in the council of God—and to hate all the Children of Darkness, each commensurate with his guilt and the vengeance due him from God.[112]

What if the Jews and Romans could stop the fighting? What if they could embrace in peace? What if the mentality of division could just drop and there were no more enemies, no more this side or that side? What if instead of cursing those on the other side that you blessed them? What of instead of hating back those who hate you that you do good for them? What if they abuse you and persecute you and you pray for them? Would that be cowardly? Would that be defeat? Would that be turning your back on your religion, on the "Son of David" faith? Would they call you a traitor? Would they then label you as one of the darkness? Would it matter to you if they did? All these thoughts raced in Simon's mind. How to present this to the world?

One of the Buddhists said something that stuck with Simon:

The massive clouds pour rain on all, both the great and the small. **The sunlight and moonlight shine upon the entire world, upon the good and the evil, upon the valued and the worthless**....I appear in the world like a large cloud that rains upon all of the dry withered sentient beings. This is so they can escape suffering, attain the joy of peace and assurance with the joys of this world and the joys of Extinction....At all times and for all beings I preach the Law the same way, as I would for any person....I offer a satisfied

---

[111] Matthew 5:43-44

[112] Dead Sea Scrolls Community Rule 1QS 1:9-11

> completion to the world, **as the rain spreads moisture all around, to the great and the low, to the good and the evil, to the wise and the stupid.**[113]

Jesus was like that, Simon thought, making us done with the pursuits of the world, like wars and money and status and so-called control. Extinct from that, dead to that, done with that, jaded to that. And this state of getting over it all does indeed come to people who are not prepared from a worldly perspective. Not well read, obviously, since when he first encountered Jesus he could not read. Not a deep philosopher like Ian, obviously, since he neither had the time nor the ambition to research all of the mind games of every way of thinking. Not rich, obviously, since he was just a working class peasant by the standards of the ruling elite. Jesus was offered to anyone who could directly connect and accept the intuitive input, observe the synchronicities, heed the directions of the Holy Spirit as the Nazarenes called it. This was perfection that came with no price but faith in the possibility of doing it. It turned the world upside down. The first became last and the last became first.[114] Priorities shift. Values change. What is identified as treasure becomes something completely different, something not even tangible. And with the shift of what is treasured comes a shift of the heart.[115]

There was this sense of community among the Nazarenes that propelled Jesus further than possible for solitary visionaries. They created a climate for change, a consensus for the intention to evolve into something better. It was this retreat into monastic lifestyle that was their sense of power, their sense of creating a working culture around the Jesus ideas in spite of the world as it is not being ready as a whole to embrace the ideas on the level of a nation or an international religion. In a way it was better to be a small group. Simon wondered what would get distorted and changed if this ever did take off and evolve into a large religious movement. That was beyond the scope of his day, however. What he was wondering was how to reach Edessa. His son, Jude, wanted to volunteer to be sent to Edessa, to represent Jesus to who he found there. He was sincere enough in his own way, but it could have been more about him getting really bored with Pella and wanting to move along to a more populated lifestyle. When the Buddhists announced they were departing and travelling East, Jude joined them.

---

[113] Lotus Sutra 5

[114] **Mark** 10:31

[115] Matthew 6:21

> God is a dyer. As the good dyes, which are called "true," dissolve with the things dyed in them, so it is with those whom God has dyed. Since his dyes are immortal, they become immortal by means of his colors.[116]

Dipped in God, immersed in God, not so much in the experience of any sort of ritual or any point in time when there is a change, but in acknowledging that God is all and all is made out of God and thus we are dipped into this great pool of divinity. Because of this we can claim immortality as our true nature, not as something earned or deserved, but as a fact of nature.

> You saw the Spirit, you became Spirit. You saw Christ, you became Christ. You saw the Father, you shall become Father. So in this place you see everything and do not see yourself, but in that place you do see yourself – and what you see you shall become.[117]

All them out there, all the soldiers thinking they are fighting for light and against darkness, when they look out there world is a dark place. They see chaos and become chaotic. We live on the same planet as they do. Our reality is vastly different. It is a matter of vision that paints reality, a painting that can shade over circumstance, that can intend to see the impossible, that dances with the patterns of synchronicities and protections, of intuitive urgings to flee to Pella, of dreams and symbols and myths and words with hidden meanings.

> When the pearl is cast down into the mud it becomes greatly despised? If it is anointed with balsam oil will it become more precious? But it always has value in the eyes of its owner. Compare the sons of God, wherever they may be. They still have value in the eyes of their Father.[118]

It is in the way that we look at the best-hidden qualities in ourselves and bring them out, redefine who we are, rename and label ourselves. Simon, the reed shaken in the wind, becomes Peter, the solid stone foundation of something that is going to be really really big. Mary, the flowing waters of the sea, becomes Magdala, the towering perspective of higher vision. Jesus was bringing out potential in us that we would never have supposed was there. God works in mysterious ways, it is said, and the most unlikely candidates become his greatest prophets.

---

[116] Philip 61.12-18

[117] Philip 61.29-35

[118] Philip 62.18-26

Jude no longer wanted to be called Jude, the name represented a religious tradition that he was now fleeing from, a refugee from. He adopted the name the meant man of heart, Lebbaios, but then discovered the name Thaddaios, which meant large hearted. If anything was to now be identified with, used as a personal label, it was the concept of love. To him, love was the essence and the key, for the Real God was not a force of vengeance and violence and division, but the Real God was a force of love.[119] Apart from the identification with "God is love" he had this burning vision of himself as being a mirror reflecting God, a "twin image" of God that exists with one foot in this dimension and reality and the other foot in the blessed fullness of his "Love God". Thus he found the name Didymos, which means twin, and finally the name Thomas, which is Greek for twin.[120] He took my horse, my old friend, the one that Mary rode to Pella on, and one morning got up at dawn and rode off into the sunrise toward Edessa.

In his own way Jude, the last we would have suspected to have become so enthused about the Jesus movement, the little boy obsessed with money and business, the little boy that thought his grandmother Mary and his father Simon had both completely lost their minds, would become the great light shining in the East. I never saw him again after that, but I hear that he built up a thriving community in Edessa before traveling on to India.

---

[119] 1 John 4:8

[120] Thomas introduction

Mark to Alexandria

What Jesus presented was a collective mind, a consensus, an agreed upon vision and intention and way of speaking and interacting and dealing with life. There were lots of group minds out there, one was currently influenced by some very scary and influential instigators that have equated support of the revolution with God and prophecy and Messianic expectations and patriotism to the dream of Jewish autonomy in a world overrun by the Romans. There were legions of Roman soldiers -- one even came through Pella recently -- acting as a collective. So having an agreed upon directive wasn't a new thing. Having Jesus being the focal point was what made it different. Having this Holy Spirit within was what made it special. It was as if each of us had an inner source to drink from. [121] We could and did learn from each other, but that was secondary from learning from the great Teacher within that made sense out of ordinary moments in life and brought to them divine meaning and purpose. It was a taking a handle on the control of life. While most are being tossed about by the storms, Jesus is for us the rudder to steer by, the ability to stay on course. All of the calmings of the storms back in Bethsaida were Jesus trying to explain this to Simon.

Every Revolution has an Opposition. What was preventing the Jews from ruling their own land was the Romans who also wanted to rule. Wrapped up in religious fanatical terms, the Sons of Darkness were opposing the Sons of Light, Satan was opposing the Messiah Son of David, Evil was opposing Good. What was the Opposition to the Revolution of Jesus? It wasn't a battle between some imagined Armageddon scope Good vs. Evil. It was Knowing vs. Ignorance, those who had the experience in the midst of those who hadn't yet had the experience. It could be stated as Light vs. Darkness, but in reality Darkness is not a thing in itself, it is just a lack of Light. If you light a lamp, the Darkness is non-existent. As long as you keep fueling the lamp, there is Light. Jesus was like that, the hope and empowerment of Light for a darkened world. The way to turn on Jesus and keep the Light shining is for each of us to keep our own personal lights burning. [122] The greater the concentration of lamps burning for Jesus in any given place, the less likely that Darkness can ever be seen again. Only the Light is real, and those who have direct experience of this fact can rest in this knowledge. Darkness goes away like a bad dream disappears once dawn comes and we awaken. Jesus is like that.

Mark had a specific and unique vision of Jesus, at least as far as any of us had encountered before. He was fascinated with interviewing Simon and gathering his stories of storms and

----

[121] John 4:14 , John 7:38

[122] Matthew 5:16

ships and such, but it was just to add to a story he was working on long before we arrived in Pella. Perhaps it was a reaction to the war going on and the expected hatred of the Romans along with the concept of the "Son of David" Messiah that was supposed to arrive and kill the Romans and drive them forever away from the promised land. Mark had a vision of the "Son of Adam" Jesus that encountered the Romans and was killed by them. It sounded very strange at first, but Mark was so passionate about his vision that he had written it into a story. He was convinced that there were references to his story in Jewish scriptures that he collected for the project. In good Nazarene style, he saw hidden meanings even in his own compositions, and saw this Jesus dying experience as symbolic of the spiritual death that each mystic must endure in order to advance.

Leave it all behind – Bethsaida, the boat, the store, the ambitions, memories, desires, dreams, fears, prejudices. It was like Mark's vision of giving up and letting them crucify you, think they've beaten you, think they've won, then after you stop breathing, stop moving, stop living, stop trusting in any God out there that has forsaken you, they entomb you and post a guard to make sure you are good and dead. But you come back to life, you unwrap the grave clothes, you escape the tomb, you live again and you are so transformed that even your friends don't recognize you, transfigured, ascended, resurrected, renewed. You prove that they cannot hold you down, defeat you. Jesus just overlaps their dimension, appears to be one of them. He blinds their dull minds to where they don't even notice that it is really Simon who is carrying the cross.[123] Jesus is really of another dimension, one they cannot kill, one they cannot defeat, one they cannot control. Simon must die so that Jesus can resurrect in his place. That is the real mystery.

> And he said to me, "Be strong, for you are the one to whom these mysteries have been given, to know them through revelation, that he whom they crucified is the first-born, and the home of demons, and the stony vessel in which they dwell, of Elohim, of the cross which is under the Law. But he who stands near him is the living Savior, the first in him, whom they seized and released, who stands joyfully looking at those who did him violence, while they are divided among themselves. Therefore he laughs at their lack of perception, knowing that they are born blind. So then the one susceptible to suffering shall come, since the body is the substitute. But what the released was my incorporeal body. But I am the intellectual Spirit filled with radiant light. He whom you saw coming to me is our intellectual Pleroma, which unites the perfect light with my Holy Spirit.[124]

---

[123] Mark 15:21

[124] Apocalypse of Peter 82.17 – 83.15

How indeed does Jesus both sit at the right hand of the Father and walk the dusty streets of Bethsaida? How does he live in Pella and die in Jerusalem? It is because Jesus is both Son of God and Son of Man, with one foot in the Pleroma and one foot in the Kosmos. The Pythagoreans had this symbol where two circles were drawn and the edge of each touched the center of the other and the symbol of a fish formed where the two overlapped. This is the mystery of the Trinity, there is that Other Circle, that alien God the Father, the Silence, of another Dimension, the Pleroma beyond the universes, can't get there even if you could ride Ezekiel's flying throne vision or Elijah's chariot. Our Circle is the tangible "real" world that we call home, a reality we taste and touch and interact with. What the Nazarenes considered with their "Jesus" was that the "fish in the middle" is like a bridge, like a portal, the Child of that Realm Beyond, that Pleroma (completeness) and also a Child of Who We Are. The idea was if we can use "Jesus" to grab into that Other Circle, and overlap some Light into our relative darkness, that we can then channel the Energy being received and make for Evolutionary Changes in our own circle, which they called the Holy Ghost, the Sacred Wind blowing from the Father through the Son and through us.[125] Now the one circle is God and the other circle is each of us, is me and is you. What this means is that the fish in the overlap for me is different from the fish in the overlap for you. I have to find my inner Jesus and you have to find your inner Jesus. It is the same connection, the same bridge to the same place, but it is individually plugged into. It is like eating. I can't eat your food for you. We can share a meal, but you will have to eat for yourself. Jesus is like this. You have to participate in the connection. Everyone has it within them, but not everyone takes advantage of it. Not everyone has faith in it enough to experience it.

There was this concept that belief in the resurrected Jesus brings salvation. Jake added the idea to Mark's Jesus story of Jesus leaving the Jerusalem tomb behind and appearing to his disciples in a far away mountain where he had previously arranged for them to go to. It was only there that they experienced the resurrected Jesus, the Jesus that the Romans could not kill and Jerusalem could not entomb. The far away mountain was of course code for Pella, which they were careful not to name in their writings. If the world knew, they may no longer enjoy their safe haven. The news came of the Temple having fallen, the revolution defeated. The keepers of the sacred texts had them hidden in caves to preserve them for saner times. The Temple was supposed to be this eternal symbol. The texts were supposed to be this living word of God. The Temple can be destroyed, the sacred texts lost, but Jesus cannot be killed off. This was the good news that Mark wanted to share with the world. The most open to such ideas of any large group of people that Mark could possibly think of was the eclectic Jewish communities in Alexandria, Egypt. They were already used to looking for hidden meanings and revelations from scripture study, and Mark's extracting the story of the

---

[125] John 3:8

rejection and death of Jesus in Jerusalem was along the lines of how they interpreted the sacred texts. After the dust and blood had settled from the war, Mark left for Alexandria. Jake continued working on his story, adding more personal memories of events and ideas from Bethsaida with Simon to Pella with the Nazarenes and traveling Buddhists. His vision was that Jesus was the living speaker for the best of the ideas presented from Jewish writings. His life quest was to write the perfect "Sermon on the Mount" having Jesus teach a concise and complete set of truths and values, collected from his notes throughout the years.

One Jewish writing that especially inspired Jake was that of the wisdom of Jesus Sirach.

> Anger yells out. Jealousy sobs. Envy snips. Insecurity criticizes. Frustration screams. A truly compassionate heart speaks comforting words. A truly caring soul speaks helpful words.
>
> The orchard of trees is judged by its fruit the same as a person's feelings are judged by his words.[126]
>
> As the Law has spoken, give charity to The Poor. Do not let The Poor leave without their needs in hand. Better to spend your money on a good brother than to leave it under a rock to rust away. Use your money as the Most High has commanded and you will find a treasure worth more than gold. Stock up your store-rooms with charity, and you will be protected from misfortune.[127]
>
> Forgive your neighbor's wrongs and when you pray your wrongs will be forgiven. If anyone holds anger against another, how then can compassion be gained from the Lord?[128]
>
> The orchard of trees is judged by its fruit the same as a person's feelings are judged by his words.[129]

The Buddhists had left a lasting impression on Jake. At times he could think of Jesus saying Buddhist thoughts easier than saying Jewish thoughts. Since Jesus was "Son of Adam" it

---

[126] Sirach 27:6

[127] Sirach 29:9-12

[128] Sirach 28:2-3

[129] Sirach 27:6

didn't matter, he was all-inclusive, spanning cultures and ages and languages. The "Son of David" Messiah never showed up. Even if you say "Son of Israel", you have limited yourself, limited your answer, limited your Jesus. If you say "Son of Abraham", you have limited yourself. Even if you say "Son of Seth", you still exclude and limit. That is why Jesus was nothing short of being "Son of Adam", child of humanity, son of man. And if "Son of Adam" and you could extract his life from Jewish scriptures, you could also find him in Homer's stories, in Pythagorean philosophy, in Stoic values, and in Buddhist gems of timeless wisdom.

> Nothing in this world is lasting. Don't think of possessions as being stones. Think of them like foamy bubbles, shimmering and then evaporating. You must learn to quickly let go of it all and go along your way.[130]
>
> The greedy do not make it to heaven, those fools who shun charity. The wise who give freely will find much happiness for eternity.[131]
>
> Though one possess hundreds of thousands of worldly possessions, one is still subject to death. All collections will be dispersed. All pile ups will be thrown down. All assemblies will be taken apart. All life must end in death.[132]
>
> It is like a great foundry with countless golden statues. Foolish people look at the outside and see only the darkened earthen molds. The master foundryman estimates that they have cooled, and opens them to extract their contents. All impurity is removed and the features clearly revealed. With my Buddha vision I see that all sentient beings are like this. Within the mud shell of passions, all have the Tathagata-nature. By means of adamantine wisdom, we break the mold of the klesas and reveal the tathagatagarbha, like pure, shining gold. Just as I have seen this and so instructed all the bodhisattvas, so should you accept it, and convert in turn all other beings.[133]
>
> It is just like what happens when gold is submerged in impure waste, where no one can see it. But someone with supernatural vision sees it and tells people about it, saying, 'If you get it out and wash it clean, you may do with it as you will,' which causes their relatives and family all to rejoice. The Well-departed One's vision is like this. He sees

---

[130] Lotus Sutra 18

[131] Dhammapada 13:11

[132] Udanavarga 1:21-22

[133] Tathagatagarbha Sutra

that for all kinds of beings, the Tathagata nature is not destroyed, though it is submerged in the muddy silt of klesas. So he appropriately expounds the Dharma and enables them to manage all things, so that the klesas covering the Buddha nature are quickly removed and beings are purified.[134]

It is like a store of treasure inside the house of an impoverished man. The owner is not aware of it, nor can the treasure speak. For a very long time it is buried in darkness, as there is no one who can tell of its presence. When you have treasure but do not know of it, this causes poverty and suffering. When the buddha eye observes sentient beings, it sees that, although they transmigrate through the five realms of reincarnation, there is a great treasure in their bodies that is eternal and unchanging. When he sees this, the Buddha teaches on behalf of all beings, enabling them to attain the treasure-store of wisdom, and the great wealth of widely caring for one another. If you believe what I have taught you about all having a treasure store, and practice it faithfully and ardently, employing skillful means, you will quickly attain the highest path.[135]

Andy had an insight about the story of life and death and how Mark's story of dying is an important part of the quest for Life:

Save the part of you that can last. Seek it out and speak from within it. When you are striving through it, everything will be in harmony for you.[136]

You are from the Fullness and you live in the realm of emptiness.[137]

When the living part detaches from the dying part then the living part can be called upon.[138]

Seeking out Life is the true treasure. The gold and silver of the world are only misleading.[139]

---

[134] Tathagatagarbha Sutra

[135] Tathagatagarbha Sutra

[136] Dialogue of the Saviour 44

[137] Dialogue of the Saviour 55

[138] Dialogue of the Saviour 57

Jake agreed and summarized in verse:

> Lay not up for yourselves treasures upon earth, where moth and rust doth corrupt, and where thieves break through and steal: But lay up for yourselves treasures in heaven, where neither moth nor rust doth corrupt, and where thieves do not break through nor steal: For where your treasure is, there will your heart be also.[140]

Andy continued:

> The lamp of the body is the psyche. As long as the inner you is kept in order, the outer you, the body, will be full of light.[141]

Jake put it into verse:

> The light of the body is the eye: if therefore thine eye be single, thy whole body shall be full of light. But if thine eye be evil, thy whole body shall be full of darkness. If therefore the light that is in thee be darkness, how great is that darkness![142]

Mary was called Magdala, which means tower, because in Pella she lived in a room on the top of the tallest building that overlooked the valley below over a cliff. The Nazarenes would visit her to learn of his famous wisdom. She was also known as the Beloved of Jesus, because of the depth of revelations she shared about the nature and meaning of Jesus. It was Mary that inspired the concepts of light and darkness, of pushing us to deeper metaphysical speculations. Mary was working on collecting her private collection of notes, ideas that she always said were spoken by Jesus and revealed not just to herself but to everyone who considers themselves to be his disciples. It was on one of those enchanting evenings in "the tower" that Mary spoke as we all sat and silently listened:

> Jesus continued again in the discourse and said unto his disciples: When I shall have gone into the Light, then herald it unto the whole world and say unto them: Cease not to seek day and night and remit not yourselves until ye find the mysteries of the Light-kingdom,

---

[139] Dialogue of the Saviour 70

[140] Matthew 6:19-21

[141] Dialogue of the Saviour 8

[142] Matthew 6:22-23

which will purify you and make you into refined light and lead you into the Light-kingdom. Renounce the whole world and the whole matter therein and all its care and all its sins, in a word all its associations which are in it, that ye may be worthy of the mysteries of the Light and be saved from all the chastisements which are in the judgments.

Renounce murmuring, renounce eavesdropping, renounce litigiousness, renounce false slander, renounce false witness, renounce pride and haughtiness, renounce belly-love, renounce babbling, renounce craftiness, renounce avarice, renounce love of the world, renounce pillage, renounce evil conversation, renounce wickedness, renounce pitilessness, renounce wrath, renounce cursing, renounce thieving, renounce robbery, renounce slandering, renounce fighting and strife, renounce all unknowing, renounce evil doing, renounce sloth, renounce adultery, renounce murder, renounce pitilessness and impiety, renounce atheism, renounce magic potions, renounce blasphemy, renounce the doctrines of error, that ye may be worthy of the mysteries of the Light and be saved from all the chastisements of the Great Dragon of the outer darkness.

Be calm, be ye loving-unto-men, be ye gentle, be ye peaceful, be ye merciful, give ye alms, minister unto the poor and the sick and distressed, be ye loving-unto-God, be ye righteous, be good, renounce all, that ye may receive the mysteries of the Light and go on high into the Light-kingdom. These are all the boundaries of the ways for those who are worthy of the mysteries of the Light.

Unto, such, therefore, who have renounced in this renunciation, give the mysteries of the Light and hide them not from them at all, even though they are sinners and they have been in all the sins and all the iniquities of the world, all of which I have recounted unto you, in order that they may turn and repent and be in the submission which I have just recounted unto you. Give unto them the mysteries of the Light-kingdom and hide them not from them at all; for it is because of sinfulness that I have brought the mysteries into the world, that I may forgive all their sins which they have committed from the beginning on. For this cause have I said unto you aforetime: 'I am not come to call the righteous.' Now, therefore, I have brought the mysteries that their sins may be forgiven for every one and they be received into the Light-kingdom. For the mysteries are the gift of the First Mystery, that he may wipe out the sins and iniquities of all sinners.[143]

Andy was having these epiphanies, these aha moments that came from the mix of having planted the seed of Jesus and having planted himself in the good soil of Pella and living with

[143] Pistis Sophia 102

the Nazarenes. Andy was a lot younger than Simon and never really concerned himself with metaphysical speculation or spiritual thoughts unless they could be practical and useful and meaningful in his daily life. What did it all mean? What were the inner Jesus encounters all about? What did it change in the one who was experiencing it? Why did Jesus push you beyond the Law? He leaves you pulled apart, alone, beyond the traditions and cultural expectations and identifications and even caring about fitting in with the structures left behind. His first aha came as an obvious thought, but it is often in the simple and obvious that the most profound truths exist:

> Everyone who has known himself has seen goodness in **everything he does**.[144]

Andy had another one of his "Andy stating the obvious" thoughts:

> The one who once sought is the one who now reveals. The one who speaks has to have first listened. The one who reveals has to have first had a vision.[145]

Jesus was like passing on a light from person to person. The initiate becomes the master. The knocker on the door becomes the opener of the door when someone else knocks. The seeker becomes the revealer. The asker becomes the answerer. It is through this cycle that the movement can outlast any of us. As long as there is a succession of those who go through and understand the experiences then it will never die out.

Andy had another insight one day:

> Now the time is at hand brothers for us to abandon our work and take a **rest**.[146]
>
> You may find rest as soon as you let go of your burdens. When you abandon that which cannot follow you, then you will find the path of rest.[147]

If they had not had left Bethsaida behind, they would not be in Pella now. You have to lighten your concerns in life, focus on what really matters. There is a sense of peace, of rest, of

---

[144] Dialogue of the Saviour 30

[145] Dialogue of the Saviour 10

[146] Dialogue of the Saviour 1

[147] Dialogue of the Saviour 66

bliss, that comes with Jesus, but this comes with the expectation, with the requirement of changing your sense of values and connections.

Andy had another insight one day:

> You are from the place where the hearts speak out of joy. In truth this is your very existence.[148]

Bethsaida is not really our hometown. Oh, that is where we were born and lived for a while, but our true home is that place of joy where Jesus lives in our hearts, the place where we really live in and come from and identify with. The part of us that was born in Bethsaida will get old and die. The part of us that is from the joyful place cannot die. That is who we really are.

Jake considered what Andy was saying. You really can't call two places home. You have to choose. All of the values and concerns back there, of having a successful business, of collecting valuable stuff, of what people think about you, of how well you fit in with where you live, was just about the god of this world, the Almighty Mammonas, which was an Aramaic way of personifying the pursuit of wealth and status.[149] For Jesus and what Jesus stands for to be your God demands that you turn your back on worshipping the Almighty Mammonas. It is in just the same way that you couldn't work full time and be dedicated to two separate jobs, you have to pick where your allegiance lies, where your true heart is. To be fat with concerns for wealth and status and to try to at the same time have a relationship with the God of Jesus would be like threading a needle with a rope.[150] It just can't be done. I guess this means that people obsessed with wealth and status can never get it. Perhaps it is not meant for them anyway.

This was a new way of thinking, way of being, way of representing. Out with the old, on with the new. You don't take new material and use it to mend some old raggedy shirt. You make a new shirt.[151] You don't make new wine from your harvest of fresh grapes and then

---

[148] Dialogue of the Saviour 34

[149] Matthew 6:24

[150] Mark 10:25

[151] Thomas 47

put it into old skins.[152] The new way of thinking requires a fresh break, a new start, a born again experience that detaches you from the old mindset.

Can you really give it ALL up? Live on nothing? Could you really become one of those wandering holy men like the Buddhists that passed through town?

> To live with the most joy, you must possess nothing. To live on such joy is to become like a glowing god.[153]
>
> The ascetics following the Sakyan son do not accept gold and silver. They renounce jewelry and gold. They have given up the use of gold and silver.[154]
>
> The requirements of life that are needed to be obtained by you who have gone forth, clothing, food, a place to rest, medicine, will be difficult to come by. These concerns did not stop me from going forth from the home life into homelessness.[155]
>
> **The wise man will act righteously, creating for him a treasure that not one can share, that no one can steal, and that cannot rust away.[156]**
>
> Happiness is living without possessions among those who possess much. Happiness is living without ties. Happiness is living without struggling among those who strive anxiously.[157]

Jake was struggling with more than one set of opposites. There were his cherished traditions of Law and Prophecy as compared with his new direct-connection to the God of Jesus. There was the life he left behind in Bethsaida with his brother and boat and home as compared with his new life here in Pella. But can this work? Is it practical? Is it something that he could honestly advise people to do if he ever got back to Bethsaida? Don't worry about life at all,

---

[152] Mark 2:22

[153] Dhammapada 15:4

[154] Gamanisamyutta 10

[155] Vanapattha Sutta 3-4

[156] Khuddakapatha 8:9

[157] Gandhari Dhammapada 167

how you will get your next meal, where your next pair of sandals will come from?[158] He did know that from his own experience that ever since he had taken the plunge and trusted in the Jesus movement with Simon that everything had worked out, at times against the odds.[159] Synchronicities had taken place that were well beyond just freak chance. They had intuitive insights of where to avoid and where to be, who to trust in and who not to trust. Here they were, wandering refugees, that were living comfortably and safe. He knew it from his experiences. Now if only his mind could wrap around the concept as being a valid one. Let go and let God. It worked in practice, but it still felt frightening.

The Buddhists had left them with the thought:

> Don't dwell on the past or live in hopes for the future. The past it is gone. The future has not yet arrived. Instead, look with insight into each presently arisen state. Know it. Be sure of it. Without thought of failure, or being shaken off course, put your effort into today. You may be dead tomorrow. No bargaining with death can hold its overwhelming arrival. But you who can live passionately and relentlessly with each present day, each present night, your death will remain a single excellent night.[160]

The way Jake translated that into his own way of thinking was:

> Take therefore no thought for the morrow: for the morrow shall take thought for the things of itself. Sufficient unto the day is the evil thereof.[161]

---

[158] Matthew 6:25

[159] Matthew 6:33

[160] Bhaddekaratta Sutta 3

[161] Matthew 6:34

Judgment and Condemnation

> Excessive in words, excessive in appearance about everyone, he who is harsh in words in condemning sinners at judgment. And his hand is the first one against him as if zeal, yet he himself is guilty of a variety of sins and intemperance.[162]

The message of Jesus was a radical one:

> Judge not, and ye shall not be judged: condemn not, and ye shall not be condemned: forgive, and ye shall be forgiven:[163]

There were several things that would get you judged and condemned in the ancient times of Israel as documented by the sacred texts.

> And the man that will do presumptuously, and will not hearken unto the priest that standeth to minister there before the LORD thy God, or unto the judge, even that man shall die: and thou shalt put away the evil from Israel.[164]

Death to those who refuse to do what they are told by those put in charge of the religion. Death to anyone who you can label as a witch.[165] Death to anyone who you can label as a medium or a wizard.[166] Utter destruction for anyone who you can label as following a different religion.[167] Death to anyone who represents the religion and gets it wrong.[168] Destruction to them, to their homes, to the people that live with them, to their cattle, to their city, and to all of their stuff.[169] You should not pity nor spare from death your own brother

---

[162] Psalms of Solomon 4:2-3

[163] Luke 6:37

[164] Deuteronomy 17:12

[165] Exodus 22:18

[166] Leviticus 20:27

[167] Exodus 22:20, 2 Chronicles 15:13

[168] Zechariah 13:3

[169] Deuteronomy 13:13-16

who has followed a different religion.[170] Death to anyone who you can label as having said anything against your definition of God.[171] Holy sites are restricted areas; unauthorized trespassers must die.[172] Holy days are serious; failure to comply with refraining from working on the Sabbath is grounds for being put to death.[173] Anyone caught being a practicing homosexual man must be put to death along with his companion.[174] Women who have engaged in premarital sex must be put to death.[175] Label and divide everyone into those who sincerely stand for the religion and those who do not, marking those who do not as candidates for extermination, young and old, even virgin girls, even boy children.[176] Leave behind desolation with no survivors and curse anyone who refuses to help you with the bloodbath.[177] The granting of the promised land came with the understanding that the chosen people kill and destroy everything in their path.[178]

It was this well documented and repeated battle hymn mentality that was woven through Jewish tradition like a plague of demonic possession insanity. It was this obsession with killing as a sacred duty that fueled the current war. The Jesus "judge not" came as a strong slap at the system. It was being irreligious, unpatriotic, disrespectful of tradition, dangerous. Then "condemn not" meant that you would have to be open minded and embrace diversity, stop being narrow minded and stop trying to identify and control the moralities of those around you. We are all in this thing together called life and there will be times when some folks get things wrong and times when we get things wrong, but if we can learn to be forgiving, we can learn to be forgiven. If we can learn to accept that most everyone is trying to do their best, then they could look at us with the same assumption.

----

[170] Deuteronomy 13:6-8

[171] Leviticus 24:16

[172] Numbers 1:51

[173] Exodus 31:15

[174] Leviticus 20:13

[175] Deuteronomy 22:19-20

[176] Ezekiel 9:4-6

[177] Jeremiah 48:9-10

[178] Judges 20:48

> *For with what judgment ye judge, ye shall be judged*: and with what **measure ye mete**, it shall be measured to you again.[179]

The "what measure ye mete" saying was just a way of expressing "what goes around comes back around" and "the love you take is equal to the love you make" way of thinking. If you are stuck in a mental state in which you judge and measure the worth of everyone out there, probe into their private lives and try to find something to point a finger at, your world and thus your life is a place filled with evils and perversions. It becomes an "us vs. them" world of the few that conform to and abide by the self-imposed set of rules looking out at a world painted as dark and fallen and consumed by sin. People become naughty by nature, depraved, in need of salvation. But if you change the lens through which you look out and try to see the good in people, try to give them the benefit of the doubt, try to overlook the differences in values, then you find that the more slack you cut them the more slack they cut you.

> Jesus said, "You see the sliver in your friend's eye, but you don't see the timber in your own eye. When you take the timber out of your own eye, then you will see well enough to remove the sliver from your friend's eye."[180]

Now there is such a thing as seeing straight and having a clear view of What Is as it is and seeing the big picture and noticing the problems enough to do something about them. So this part of judgment is required. We have to distinguish between smart and stupid, between correct construction and faulty workmanship. It is easy to think that any problem is someone else's fault and that we are perfect. You see some little obstacle in their vision, something they need to correct to achieve your definition of perfect, and you get sunk into this perpetual drone of being critical. Usually the overly critical people have even bigger blockages to their own vision that they don't see are there because they are too busy finding fault with others.

> Give not that which is holy unto the dogs, neither cast ye your pearls before swine, lest they trample them under their feet, and turn again and rend you.[181]

---

[179] Matthew 7:2

[180] Thomas 26

[181] Matthew 7:6

Another part of judgment is to discern if people are ready for being taught about spiritual metaphysical truths and values. Jesus said that if you take your most treasured and sacred holy object and give it to a dog, it will get carried away and left abandoned and dirty and shat upon.[182] And if you hang an expensive pearl necklace on a pig, it will not only not be appreciated, you may get attacked for annoying the pig.

> The way of life is this: first, you shall love the God who made you; second, your neighbor as yourself, and **whatever you would not have done to you, do not do to another**.[183]

If your life is directed with an empathetic compassion for What Is, and this compassion is directed to those around you, then the result is that you put yourself in their place. You see yourself in their position. You walk a mile in their sandals. If you were to judge and measure and assess the value of other people as if you were judging and measuring and assessing the value of yourself, you would proceed differently than the harsh fundamentalist narrow-minded types. This is the way that Jesus replaced the Law of Moses with the Law of Love.

---

[182] Thomas 93

[183] Didache 1:2

Narrow Path

> **Stand at the corner and observe, asking for the old and narrow path. Take that path and find rest for your souls.** But they said they would not take that path.[184]

The simple and the obvious are obscured from the world. The simple walk in the woods reveals experiences that are unknown in the city. The wide crowded city streets with their businesses trying to maximize their profits, with its hurry and competition and driven quests for greed and power are meaningless on the mountain trail. Simon had learned that in his travels, his mountain climbing vision quests, his solitary side. I think we all came to appreciate the road less traveled. We all came to appreciate getting away from the noise and mental pollution of living by the busy streets of life.[185]

> Not every one that saith unto me, Lord, Lord, shall enter into the kingdom of heaven; but he that **doeth the will** of my Father which is in heaven.[186]

One big difference in Jesus as compared to the "normal" religious way of thinking is that it is not reduced to words but to actions. The busy city street is run by words, of knowing the words to say to belong to the larger group, words that identify your religion, your heritage, your allegiances. Jesus was not about "praise you, Jesus" wordplay. Jesus was about empowering real and active transformations of values and abilities and effectual impact that can be made in the world around us. Jesus was the bridge that connected us to the Father and let the Holy Spirit flow into our immediate experiences. This is our "kingdom of heaven" in that we "do God" and "become God" or awaken to the fact that because of the Holy Spirit flowing through us that we "participate" in God.

> Whosoever cometh to me, and heareth my sayings, and doeth them, I will shew you to whom he is like: He is like a man which built an house, and digged deep, and laid the foundation on a rock: and when the flood arose, the stream beat vehemently upon that house, and could not shake it: for it was founded upon a rock. But he that heareth, and doeth not, is like a man that *without a foundation* built an **house** upon the earth; against

---

[184] Jeremiah 6:16

[185] Matthew 7:13

[186] Matthew 7:21

which the stream did beat vehemently, and immediately it fell; and **the ruin of that house was great**.[187]

Jesus is a gift, a channel, an open and direct-connection to something so powerful and transformational that the potential in the experiencer is like having a strong enough foundation that no storm that the world out there can throw at us can move us. A gift has to be received. A channel has to be utilized. A connection has to be plugged into. A foundation has to be built upon.

---

[187] Luke 6:47-49

Mark's Passion

> No man can enter into a strong man's house, and spoil his goods, except he will first bind the strong man; and then he will spoil his house.[188]

If you are a strong person, you are safe in your house, you are strong, you are in control of all your stuff. There is no way they can come into your space and mess up your life unless you are stupid enough to let them waltz in your front door and willingly sit down in a chair while they tie you up with a rope. Now consider, what it is that THEY could do to you that would symbolically be tying you up and preventing you from exercising your own STRENGTH and protecting your own stuff? It is when they take away your freedom of thought and make you think like them, make you operate out of blind faith and ignore your own experiences.

> For people do not gather figs from thorns or from thorn trees, if they are wise, nor grapes from thistles. For on the one hand that which is always becoming is in that from which it is, being from what is not good, which becomes destruction for it (the soul) and death. But that (immortal soul) which comes to be in the Eternal One is in the One of the life and the immortality of the life which they resemble.[189]

To come to the end, and leave it all behind. To put to sleep in death all that was once clung to as life itself. To throw it back in their face and have them either kill you or let you be. But you know the answer. They cannot let you be. Not there. Not in their domain, in their kingdom, in their world. You are an alien to them and they must destroy you accordingly before you infect those around you with your foreign thinking and challenge the very paradigm that feeds them and gives them power. Let this cup pass from me? I think not. I embrace it. Let them crucify me, steal my stuff, lay my breathless corpse in their hollow tomb, and dare to taunt me with guards waiting at the door, ready to bonk me good if I dare wake up now. Consciousness is a wonderful force, and an aeon cannot die. They don't understand that, of course. They are but dirt, mindless drones acting out of group mind, never daring to wake up. They each exist sleeping in their own caves, having been crucified, having been nailed down until they stopped squirming, taunted until they stopped protesting, mocked until they gave up, then wrapped up tight, rolled hard and put away wet. They think they are clever and classless and free, but their world is but a matrix held up by wires and duct tape. If only they knew. If only they pushed a little and actually tried. I unwrap myself, and

---

[188] Mark 3:27

[189] Apocalypse of Peter 76:4-17

in one swift force of will power the door of the tomb forces itself open and the guards at the entrance fall into sleep, and I have risen, and not just risen, transformed, transfigured, and I know from the experience, from the mystery, that the living part of me cannot die, that they can do nothing to me now, I reach out in all directions with a sense of light and bliss that they can never know unless they are willing to unwrap themselves and dare peek out of the prison they are entombed in. I am the resurrection and the life, and this is the only way to come to the state of being What Is.

They take myth and see it as history, take symbolism and see it as literal fact, take parables and see it as real events. So if you want to teach in myth and symbolism and parables, you can reach the few that understand what you are doing and grasp the deeper meaning you are trying to convey. But for the masses, you wrap your myth in history, give flesh and blood to your vision, a time and place to your inspiration. You turn your parables into stories about your hero. You turn your visions into events. You take the highest insights of your symbolic understanding and encapsulate them into stories that they will have to think are real otherwise they won't even listen to them. They may not get it, but they can learn it and repeat it and record it and preserve it for some future generations who are insightful enough to understand the symbolism and hidden messages.

The Buddha's Dharma is like that. Dharma is subjective and relative, ideas and myths and such that can be useful tools, vehicles for experiences. The way old Buddha described it is that dharma is like coming to a river and building a raft to use to get to the other side. Once you are past the river and walking up the mountain trail on the other side you don't carry the raft with you. You leave it behind. It was good and useful and needed, but after it has served its purpose you need to stop clinging to it. So in that sense your own personal dharma is your currently held baggage of theories and calculations of how What Is really is. Now gnosis is a really old Greek word that means you learned something because you directly experienced it. You don't have blind faith in it. You didn't just learn words to repeat back. You lived it. And so, my current theory is that if you keep refining your dharma and learning from your gnosis that the more you "get", the more you notice, the more then makes sense in your little aha moments, the more that you are now prepared to experience and learn from.[190]

> Yea, his soul draweth near unto the grave, and his life to the destroyers. If there be a messenger with him, an interpreter, one among a thousand, to shew unto man his uprightness: Then he is gracious unto him, and saith, Deliver him from going down to the pit: I have found a ransom. His flesh shall be fresher than a child's: he shall return to the

---

[190] Mark 4:24

> days of his youth: He shall pray unto God, and he will be favourable unto him: and he shall see his face with joy: for he will render unto man his righteousness. He looketh upon men, and if any say, I have sinned, and perverted that which was right, and it profited me not; He will deliver his soul from going into the pit, and his life shall see the light. Lo, all these things worketh God oftentimes with man, To bring back his soul from the pit, to be enlightened with the light of the living.[191]

Ransom is a concept that fascinated Mark. If someone is a prisoner of war, you can arrange to set them free if you give their captors something that they agree is of greater value than their prisoner. Now this could be a sum of money paid for their pardon and release. Or it could be an exchange of prisoners, where one side exchanges its prisoners of war for its own soldiers that were being held prisoner by the enemy. Now what would happen if someone really great was offered in ransom for a lot of prisoners? What if there were thousands of prisoners being held by the enemy and you offered the ransom of handing over your beloved king to the enemy in exchange for setting all of the prisoners of war free? They would do it, because to hold your king captive meant that they won the war. Winning a war is either killing all of the peasants that are fighting the various battles, or it is defined as capturing the king. Interesting "what if" was going through Mark's mind. What if the king was offered in ransom in exchange for stopping the entire war? What if the ransom of offering the king was the agreement of a peace treaty?

Mark had found a couple of quotes that haunted him. Even the being imprisoned by death could somehow be ransomed. Even the state of being damned by God could be ransomed. If Jesus was the greatest force in the cosmos linked to the Highest Power, then what if Jesus himself was to be ransomed?

> I will ransom them from the power of the grave; I will redeem them from death: O death, I will be thy plagues; O grave, I will be thy destruction: repentance shall be hid from mine eyes.[192]

> Be merciful to your people, and let our punishment suffice for them. Make my blood their purification, and take my life in exchange for theirs.[193]

---

[191] Job 33:22-30

[192] Hosea 13:14

What if the "Son of Adam" himself came down to us to help us, to offer his life in ransom for all of ours? It could save us from the Romans. It could save us from death. It could save us from whatever powers that be there are that think they rule this dimension, this cosmos, this world, and try to chain us and hold us down.

> And whosoever of you will be the chiefest, shall be servant of all. For even the Son of man came not to be ministered unto, but to minister, and to give his life a ransom for many.[194]

How to symbolize this ransom? How to convey his vision that Jesus was greater than all of the politics and religion of the world? Greater than Caesar. Greater than the highest of the high priests in Jerusalem back in the day when the Temple stood strong and they saw no end in sight. Flash back forty years to his childhood memories of visiting Jerusalem in a different age, before the war, before the organization of the revolution, before the destruction of the Temple, before the working arrangement between the Romans and the Herodian high priesthood dissolved in war.

> Christ came to ransom some, to save others, to redeem others. He ransomed those who were strangers and made them his own. And he set his own apart, those whom he gave as a pledge according to his plan. It was not only when he appeared that he voluntarily laid down his life, but he voluntarily laid down his life from the very day the world came into being. Then he came first in order to take it, since it had been given as a pledge. It fell into the hands of robbers and was taken captive, but he saved it. He redeemed the good people in the world as well as the evil.[195]

The drama of Christ giving his very life to save us is something timeless, something that happened as an event before the world came to be, in that realm of myth and spiritual skies and the setting up of fates and patterns and conflicts and solutions.

Back then Pontios Pilatos was a ruthless Roman known for persecuting Jewish and Samaritan spiritual leaders. He lived in Caesarea by the Great Sea because he disdained the Jewish religion in Jerusalem. He was so hated by the Jews that word of this reached Rome at which time the Romans removed him from office.

---

[193] 4 Maccabees 6:28-29

[194] Mark 10:44-45

[195] Philip 52.35 – 53.14

Joseph Caiaphas was high priest at a time when the office was but a puppet assigned figurehead for the masses to think that the Jewish religion still operated under its own control. In reality, they did nothing without Roman approval. When the Romans removed Pontios Pilatos from office, Joseph Caiaphas lost his position at the exact same time. He was but a playing piece in a larger game. Back then Joseph Caiaphas lived in the rich "upper city" part of Jerusalem.

This focus of a story came to mind for Mark, one so vivid that the distinction between fiction and history blurred. Once the patterns are observed and the ideas extracted and woven together, they take on a life of their own. The "must have happened that way" takes control, especially once the clues are extracted from ancient writings and the pesher lens applied.

+

Third Day

+

Abraham was journeying, willing to sacrifice his son, and the third day had arrived with the symbolic appearance of the "substitute sacrifice" that saved the son's life. It was on this third day that the death sentence on the son's life was lifted, that he lived again.

> And Abraham rose up early in the morning, and saddled his ass, and took two of his young men with him, and Isaac his son, and clave the wood for the burnt offering, and rose up, and went unto the place of which God had told him. **Then on the third day Abraham lifted up his eyes, and saw the place afar off**.[196]

On the third day, it was revealed that Jacob, Israel himself, was no longer there. The spirit of Israel had departed, fled. It seemed like a description of how Simon and company had fled.

---

[196] Genesis 22:3-4

> And Jacob stole away unawares to Laban the Syrian, in that he told him not that he fled. So he fled with all that he had; and he rose up, and passed over the river, and set his face toward the mount Gilead. And it was told Laban **on the third day that Jacob was fled**.[197]

It was the story of David that caught Mark's eyes the most. It speaks of battle and defeat, of escape and appearing still living while so many are fallen and dead.

> It came even to pass on **the third day**, that, behold, **a man** came out of the camp from Saul with his clothes rent, and earth upon his head: and so it was, when he came to David, that he fell to the earth, and did obeisance. And David said unto him, From whence comest thou? And he said unto him, **Out of the camp of Israel am I escaped**. And David said unto him, How went the matter? I pray thee, tell me. And he answered, That **the people are fled from the battle, and many of the people also are fallen and dead**; and Saul and Jonathan his son are dead also.[198]

The promise in *Hosea*, which is another way of saying *Joshua*, the equivalent of the name *Jesus*, was very appropriate in the aftermath of war and escaping refugees, and renewal of hope.

> Come, and let us return unto the LORD: for he hath torn, and he will heal us; he hath smitten, and he will bind us up. After two days will he revive us: **in the third day he will raise us up, and we shall live in his sight**. Then shall we know, if we follow on to know the LORD: his going forth is prepared as the morning; and he shall come unto us as the rain, as the latter and former rain unto the earth.[199]

Jesus, the Son of Adam, was not only rejected by and sentenced by the religion, he was disrespected and condemned by the politics. But no matter to what extreme he was forbidden to be a part of their world, the end result was that they did not and could not destroy him. They mock him, but he attains glory. They beat him, but he acquires the strength that is beyond their comprehension. They disrespect him and make sure that he is not a part of, not a supporter of, not a representative of, the religion of the chief priests. They kill him, but they are the ones that end up dead. They hand him over to the Romans, but they are the ones that

---

[197] Genesis 31:20-22

[198] 2 Samuel 1:2-4

[199] Hosea 6:1-3

the Romans destroyed. They give their verdict from their Temple, and now there is not one stone to be left on top of another. They thought they crucified Jesus to a ignoble death, but what they did was crucify themselves in their failed revolution.

> Saying, Behold, we go up to Jerusalem; and the **Son of man** shall be delivered unto the chief priests, and unto the scribes; and they shall condemn him to death, and shall deliver him to the Gentiles: And they shall mock him, and shall scourge him, and shall spit upon him, and shall kill him: and **the third day he shall rise again**.[200]

Now what crazy talk is this that we should identify with the one who was rejected, follow in his footsteps, be willing to throw ourselves at the establishments at hand and see that they can't kill the eternal part of us? We have to take that plunge of faith, of becoming dead to them and having them become dead to us.

> And when he had called **the people** unto him **with his disciples** also, he said unto them, Whosoever will come after me, let him deny himself, and take up his cross, and follow me. For whosoever will save his life shall lose it; but whosoever shall lose his life for my sake *and the gospel's*, the same shall save it. For what shall it profit a man, if he shall gain the whole world, and lose his own soul? Or what shall a man give in exchange for his soul?[201]

There is a fear in the establishments. It is a fear of anyone trying to shift the paradigm, rock the boat, make waves, question how things are controlled. They want to manipulate with money, with power, with imposing fears of punishment, of death, of hell. Something like Jesus had to be suppressed. If people could direct-connect to What Is, where would that leave the priesthood? Where would that leave the whole system of religion? If people become internally inspired, what will they need the sacred texts for? If people sincerely experience transformational changes that they can define and express, what will they need sacrifices and rituals and all of the visible indicators of belonging to the religion? No. Jesus must die. And all who think like Jesus must die. They must not be allowed to infect the sheep like some stray wolves.

What protected Jesus from being under the control of their punishment, of their imposed death, of their threatened hell? Mary had anointed him with the sacred oil; Simon was witness. She was his hope, his counterpart, his one that he saved and his savior. It was as if

---

[200] Mark 10:33-34

[201] Mark 8:34-37

he was Osiris and she was his Isis, making sure that death did not win over her beloved. Like Cybele with Attis, or Ishtar with Tammuz, or Anath with Baal, or Aphrodite with Adonis, the pattern of thought permeated the sacred landscape of Mark's time. Mark saw his Jesus as fulfilling the Mysteries, perfecting the Zodiac, living out the prophecies, taking his place in the cosmopolitan mixture of spiritual traditions. At last a Jewish story could thrive and be appreciated in such a philosophical city as Alexandria. The story was ripe for the telling, it just had to be laid out and presented in the way that everyone expected such a story to be. Jesus had to be a hero, a living god that had control over nature and circumstance, a miracle worker, a healer. Jesus had to be strong enough to stand up against the establishment, against the culture, against traditions. Jesus had to face the fears and even face the persecution, the taunting, the disrespect, the being a forsaken outcast from the puppet charade of society. Jesus had to run head on into letting them destroy him, and in doing so ensure his immortality.

The Romans would like that Jesus is in effect the anti-Messiah, the opposite of the Son of David of the Revolutionaries. He could be retrojected back to before the war, standing in the Temple when it was still there, preaching peace and prophesizing the fate of those who remained to fight when the "Son of Man" Titus came to town. Did "Jesus" belong to the Romans even more so than to the Jews? Placed back 40 years before the Temple fell, Jesus became the voice of reason crying out in a sea of revolutionary madness, warning the Jews that they will not win, and promising the world that true spirituality transcended the grasps of one small group of people on a much larger planet. He was a product of Jewish metaphysical spirituality, but was easier assimilated by foreigners than by the Jews themselves.

> He saith unto him the third time, Simon, son of Jonas, lovest thou me? Peter was grieved because he said unto him the third time, Lovest thou me? And he said unto him, Lord, thou knowest all things; thou knowest that I love thee. Jesus saith unto him, Feed my sheep. Verily, verily, I say unto thee, When thou wast young, thou girdedst thyself, and walkedst whither thou wouldest: but when thou shalt be old, thou shalt stretch forth thy hands, and another shall gird thee, and carry thee whither thou wouldest not.[202]

Simon wasn't sure of Mark's vision and plan. Jesus was being used for a political agenda, given a time and place to live and have been some 40 years in the past. Expedient means, Mark explained, a vehicle for teaching higher truths that the masses cannot be expected to grasp any other way. They have to have a Jesus that they can reach out and touch, not a

---

[202] John 21:17-18

vision walking on water alone. Mystics love visions and metaphysical speculation, but the average person out there needs a story that is tangible and real to them. What does it matter to you that Jesus spent time in Jerusalem? That God forsaken place, Simon answered, why not just send him for a three-day tour of Hades? Listen, Mark calmly explained, the revolution failed, but that will only fuel the fire of another revolution. Mark my words; within a hundred years the Son of David Messiah mentality will rear its ugly head again.[203] We have a chance here to change the world. We can present Jesus as an alternative to the Messianic hopes. His is the Spirit of peace and compassion, openness to diversity, a non-judgmental acceptance of what is becoming a cosmopolitan world. If people rally around Jesus instead of the next Messianic pretender that wants to fulfill the xenophobic prophecies of God-backed war, then it will be worth it. Anyways, the true knowers will be able to see the symbolism of the story the same way that we see the symbolisms behind the stories of ancient scriptures. I will be careful to detail your stories and truths and weave them into my vision of Jerusalem having killed their only hope and having Him resurrect into the greatest spiritual force the Age of Pisces will ever know. Trust me, Jesus will be bigger than Mithras. He fulfils the circuit of the Zodiac. He fulfils the prophecies from the Jewish scriptures. He teaches the greatest truths, and especially that of peace. God knows the world could use peace. If you fight fire with fire, everyone gets burned. You become what you are trying to defeat. You have to outsmart the system, form a counter-culture, create a movement. Ghost stories are not powerful enough to do that, Simon. So Simon agreed to venture to Alexandria and join Mark on his world changing "good news" project.

---

[203] The Simon bar Kokhba revolt lasted from 132 to 135. Simon thought of himself as the Messiah. Hadrian defeated Simon and his rebellion, forbidding Jews from entering Jerusalem, which he had renamed Aelia Capitolina. It was in the aftermath of that defeat of Messianic Judaism that Christianity began to grow as an alternative religion.

JEWISH REVOLUTIONARIES AGAINST THE ROMAN EMPIRE

66 ALEXANDRIA UPRISING
   JERUSALEM: JEWS TAKE CONTROL
CHRISTIANS FLEE WAR AND GO TO
PELLA (PER EUSEBIUS)
67 VESPASIAN AND TITUS
   SECURE CONTROL OF GALILEE
68 JERUSALEM TEMPLE CONTROLLED
   BY ZEALOTS, CITY BY SICARII
69 VESPASIAN AND TITUS
   SECURE CONTROL OF JUDAEA
70 JERUSALEM WALLS KNOCKED DOWN
   CITY BURNED, TEMPLE DESTROYED
↳ OVER ONE MILLION PEOPLE KILLED ↲
115-117 KITOS WAR
   JEWS DESTROY TEMPLES, SET FIRES
   IN CYRENE, CYPRUS, EGYPT, LIBYA
130 HADRIAN REBUILDS JERUSALEM
   RENAMED "AELIA CAPITOLINA"
132 SIMON BAR KOKHBA (BEN KOSHIBA)
   LEADS REBELLION AS MESSIAH
135 HADRIAN REGAINS ROMAN
   CONTROL OF JERUSALEM
   JEWS FORBIDDEN IN CITY.

+

Archon of the Kosmos

+

> Now is the judgment of this world: now shall **the prince of this world** be cast out. And I, if I be lifted up from the earth, will draw all men unto me. [204]

The Greek for "prince of this world" is "archon of this kosmos", lord of this dimension, the demiurge for this universe. What was cast out and judged was not Caesar, not the Romans. What was thrown away was the Jerusalem Temple, the high priesthood, the sacrifices of animals, the ability for the xenophobia of the judgmental self-righteousness to gain enough power to persecute those who didn't fit in. What was thrown out was the very "God" of Jerusalem, or it may be better to say it as the very projection and conceptualization of "God" as it was in Jerusalem. This "God" had stood for the conquest of the Holy Land, the stealing it from the people who lived there before, the death of those who stood in the way, the destruction of that which was valued by those who got pushed aside. The "prince of this world" was fallen from his high tower, replaced by a merciful and forgiving and peace loving Father of Jesus. Revolution.

> Truth is one single thing; it is many things and for our sakes to teach about this one thing in love through many things. The Rulers wanted to deceive **Man**, since they saw that he had a kinship with those that are truly good. [205]

Now some thought that this meant that Jesus was not really Jewish at all, that his Father was not the "God" of the Jews. This was true in a way, but with the thought that the "God" of the Jews that supported the Temple cult in Jerusalem was not representing the original "God" of Judaism, the "God" of Judah, of Israel, of Abraham, of Enoch, of Seth, of Adam. There was this metaphysical quest to get back to the original, to the core, to the "What Is God" before religion and politics had corrupted him in the human mind and heart. People can get really

---

[204] John 12:31-32

[205] Philip 54.15-21

perverted concepts of "God" in mind and with such justify bigotries, persecutions, wars, revolutions, invasions, tortures, witch hunts, cold wars, manifest destinies, controlling people using fear tactics, and other such atrocities. Now if the real "God" had seen how misrepresented he had become, how degraded, how perverted, how used as an excuse for greed and violence to reign, wouldn't he want to put an end to it all? That was Mark's take on it. It was the "Real God" getting mad that put an end to the Temple in Jerusalem, to the control of the Jewish high priesthood, to the war spirit that Judaism had been deprecated into. It may have been a death blow to Judaism in its guise of Messianic speculation and prophesy, but it was the birth of the extraction of the "Jesus" prophecies and hopes and dreams.

Therefore thou shalt speak unto them this word; Thus saith the LORD God of Israel, Every bottle shall be filled with wine: and they shall say unto thee, Do we not certainly know that every bottle shall be filled with wine? Then shalt thou say unto them, Thus saith the LORD, Behold, I will fill all the inhabitants of this land, even the kings that sit upon David's throne, and the priests, and the prophets, and **all the inhabitants of Jerusalem, with drunkenness**. And I will dash them one against another, even the fathers and the sons together, saith the LORD: I will not pity, nor spare, nor have mercy, but destroy them. Hear ye, and give ear; be not proud: for the LORD hath spoken. Give glory to the LORD your God, before he cause darkness, and before your feet stumble upon the dark mountains, and, while ye look for light, he turn it into the shadow of death, and make it gross darkness. But if ye will not hear it, my soul shall weep in secret places for your pride; and mine eye shall weep sore, and run down with tears, because the LORD'S flock is carried away captive. Say unto the king and to the queen, Humble yourselves, sit down: for your principalities shall come down, even the crown of your glory.[206]

Mark invented a character based on the Jewish Sicarii group that was the most violent edge of the revolution, naming him "Judas Iscariot". And why did this Judas betray Jesus to the Religion? It was for money. It was for greed. They wanted to rule the world and defeat and rob the Romans? They sold out their only hope for a very temporal paltry sum of fleeting victories and status that would end in famine and defeat.

Then said Jesus again unto them, I go my way, and ye shall seek me, and shall die in your sins: whither I go, ye cannot come. Then said the Jews, Will he kill himself? Because he saith, Whither I go, ye cannot come. And he said unto them, Ye are from beneath; I am

---

[206] Jeremiah 13:12-18

> from above: ye are of this world; I am not of this world. I said therefore unto you, that ye
> shall die in your sins: for if ye believe not that I am *he*, ye shall die in your sins.[207]

The time to follow has ended. Once the war was in full swing, no one was allowed to leave for such a peaceful haven as Pella. They made their revolution; now let them die in it.

✝

New Passover

✝

There is this concept of food and drink that will make you immortal, ambrosia of the gods of Olympus. Jesus offers this meal and he himself partakes of this meal, a protection to ensure awakening.

> Thereafter there cometh a receiver of the little Sabaoth, the Good, him of the Midst. He himself bringeth a cup filled with thoughts and wisdom, and soberness is in it; and he handeth it to the soul. And they cast it into a body which can neither sleep nor forget because of the cup of soberness which hath been handed unto it; but it will whip its heart persistently to question about the mysteries of the Light until it find them, through the decision of the Virgin of Light, and inherit the Light for ever.[208]

The ancient children of Israel found themselves in a hostile desert, facing uncertainties and death. Out of desperation comes hope. Out of death in truth comes life. The LORD Jesus feeds himself and us with the sacred bread, the cup of wisdom, the strength to endure anything we have to go though, knowing that we will awaken immortal.

---

[207] John 8:21-24

[208] Pistis Sophia 147

And when the children of Israel saw it, they said one to another, It is manna: for they wist not what it was. And Moses said unto them, This is the bread which the LORD hath given you to eat.[209]

Then Jesus said unto them, Verily, verily, I say unto you, Except ye eat the flesh of the Son of man, and drink his blood, ye have no life in you. Whoso eateth my flesh, and drinketh my blood, hath eternal life; and I will raise him up at the last day. For my flesh is meat indeed, and my blood is drink indeed. He that eateth my flesh, and drinketh my blood, dwelleth in me, and I in him. As the living Father hath sent me, and I live by the Father: so he that eateth me, even he shall live by me. This is that bread which came down from heaven: not as your fathers did eat *manna*, and are dead: he that eateth of this bread shall live for ever.[210]

It is interesting that the new "Passover" meal is not meat, not a dead animal. Jesus replaced the meal with what he identifies as his body and blood, but he is speaking symbolically, presenting bread and wine to the disciples. As he was to transfigure into light, so the bread and wine transubstantiated into his body and blood. This became a ritual of bloodless sacrifice that could be performed by Nazarenes in order to "seal" themselves for the "New Passover" and be protected from the fate of those outcast from the New Jerusalem. To die in old Jerusalem was bad, but to be "dead" in New Jerusalem was a death that meant more.

[209] Exodus 16:15

[210] John 6:53-58

+

Mount of Olives

+

And one shall say unto him, What are these wounds in thine hands? Then he shall answer, Those with **which I was wounded in the house of my friends**. Awake, O sword, against my shepherd, and against the man that is my fellow, saith the LORD of hosts: **smite the shepherd, and the sheep shall be scattered**:[211] and I will turn mine hand upon the little ones. And it shall come to pass, that in all the land, saith the LORD, two parts therein shall be cut off and die; but the third shall be left therein. And I will bring the third part **through the fire**, and will refine them as silver is refined, and will try them as gold is tried: they shall call on my name, and I will hear them: I will say, It is my people: and they shall say, The LORD is my God. Behold, the day of the LORD cometh, and thy spoil shall be divided in the midst of thee. **For I will gather all nations against Jerusalem to battle; and the city shall be taken,** and the houses rifled, and the women ravished; and half of the city shall **go forth into captivity**, and the residue of the people shall not be cut off from the city. Then shall the LORD go forth, and fight against those nations, as when he fought in the day of battle. And **his feet shall stand in that day upon the mount of Olives**, which is before Jerusalem on the east, and the mount of Olives shall cleave in the midst thereof toward the east and toward the west, and there shall be a very great valley; and **half of the mountain shall remove toward the north, and half of it toward the south**. And ye shall flee to the valley of the mountains; for the valley of the mountains shall reach unto Azal: yea, **ye shall flee**, like as ye fled from before the earthquake in the days of Uzziah king of Judah: and the LORD my God shall come, and all the saints with thee.[212]

How to change the world? It was not by hoping for some Messiah to fly out of the sky on the clouds and blast his way through all the problems at hand. It was not by just sitting back and complaining and praying and hoping things get better. Movements took movers. The revolutionaries acted in group-mind with their violent plans and organizations. The Jesus

---

[211] Mark 14:27

[212] Zechariah 13:6-14:5

movement has to act though a network of like-minded people. The experience can be contagious, passed from those who know to those who want to know. The words can be planted as seeds in receptive minds, inspiring them to change themselves and thus change the world around them. Everybody wanted to become immortal, to be saved by some god, to be empowered by some externally applied grace to advance and survive. But what Jesus was all about was an empowering to partake of What Is, to channel the Divine, to breathe in and out the Holy Breath, to reach within and pull from the sacred fountain, the Connection. To become God by participation was a high ambition.

> They wanted to take the **Free Man** and make him a slave to them forever. There are powers which […] man, not wishing him to be saved, in order that they may […]. For if man is saved, there will not be any sacrifices […] and animals will not be offered to the powers. Indeed the animals were the ones to whom they sacrificed. They were indeed offering them up alive, but when they offered them up they died. As for **Man**, they offered him up to God dead, and he lived.[213]

In the Greek-speaking world, there was talk of Christ like talk of Messiah in the Hebrew-speaking world. Christ was the anointed representative of what was imagined to be the highest god, but no longer thought of as just a human that was appointed and adopted and consecrated to such a position. Christ was part of God, the Son of God, like Hercules was son of Zeus. This was the Greek world mindset, and it bled over into Jewish thought, especially in Alexandria. Simon didn't like the label Christ, it invoked images of a warring angel trying to save Jerusalem, a xenophobic cosmic dictator to come that would judge the world and take care of only a small set of the people on this planet. If Jesus was anything, it was Chrest, a similar Greek word that meant "the good one". The name Jesus itself was Greek, the name of the companion of Moses in the old stories, called Joshua in Hebrew. The two could not be more different. The original Jesus had come into the promised land, taking over the possessions of those who lived there, killing all that stood in his way. Simon's Jesus had forsaken the promised land, left it to crumble and rot, left its revolutionaries to bleed and fall, and spiraling outward away from the promised land there was hope and peace and acceptance and forgiveness. Maybe the Jesus of Moses could be called "Jesus Christ", but Simon's Jesus was "Jesus Chrest". He hated the term Christian, disdained all the Messianic narrow mindedness. If anything call us Chrestians.

---

[213] Philip 54.29 – 55.5

> But after that I am risen, I will go before you into **Galilee**.[214]

After risen, stick around in Jerusalem? Stay in Judaea? It is as Jesus is saying, when I get out of this, I'm heading back to Galilee. Judaea represented Judaism, while Galilee represented the "sea" of the Gentiles. It is symbolic that the "Christ" of Judaism would be seen again, but not among Judaism. It was the beginning of a new age for a new generation, fresh wine for new skins, new material for new fabric.

> But **Peter** said unto him, Although all shall be offended, yet will not I. And Jesus saith unto him, Verily I say unto thee, That *this day*, even in this night, before the cock crow *twice*, thou shalt deny me thrice.[215]

What was it about Simon, about "Peter" the rock, that so understood Jesus and supported Jesus and identified with Jesus and yet could find an opportunity to deny him? It was to tell the story. There is that initial "play it safe" denial phase of having encountered Jesus and known about what must be done about it, but living in fear of what others might think. It was counter culture in a judgmental world.

> And he cometh, and findeth them sleeping, and saith unto **Peter**, **Simon**, sleepest thou? couldest not thou watch one hour? Watch ye and pray, lest ye enter into temptation. The spirit truly is ready, but the flesh is weak.[216]

The world is sleeping. The few that are in the process of waking up must resist the temptation to fall back into the sleep of unknowing. It is a tension between the spiritual desire to know, to connect and to evolve beyond being tied down by the physical "reality" of fears, and wanting to continue to play the same old games and habits and prejudices.

> And **Peter followed him afar off**, even into the palace of the high priest: and he sat with the servants, and **warmed himself at the fire**.[217]

---

[214] Mark 14:28

[215] Mark 14:29-30

[216] Mark 14:37-38

[217] Mark 14:54

Now of course no stranger in town would be allowed to sit by the fire in the palace of the high priest in Jerusalem. But the symbolism was key to the story. There is this sense of immediate comfort of the palace with the warm fire surrounded by people of that same mindset, safe within the religion.

> And as Peter was beneath in the palace, there cometh **one of the maids of the high priest**: And when she saw Peter warming himself, she looked upon him, and said, And thou also wast with Jesus the **Nazarite**.[218]

It becomes obvious that you are not really one of them. You can deny and pretend for some time. In the end you will be noticed as being different, being one of the type of people who dare question, who dare want to change everything.

> We heard him say, **I will destroy this temple** that is made with hands, and within three days I will build another made without hands.[219]

Jesus is not about adding some sense of values onto the top of the existing religion, not about reforming, not about revival, not about restructuring. Jesus destroys the temple of the old religion, the touchable familiar definitions of sacred as separated from the profane. Jesus resurrects into something other, something not touchable, something not limited to expressions of objects and rituals and words and beliefs. Out with the old, in with the new. New temple. New Jerusalem. New kingdom that is not of this world. From a hand made hand written hand-controlled religion to a heart felt internally known Holy Spirit guided spirituality. And it was obvious that Simon was one of them Nazarenes, he looked like one, talked like one, held values like one, reacted like one. There was no denial that was convincing. He saw past the temporary structures of religion and looked into the future enough to see it all crumble and fail.

> And straightway in the morning the chief priests held a consultation with the elders **and scribes and the whole council**, and bound Jesus, and carried him away, and delivered him to **Pilate**.[220]

---

[218] Mark 14:66-67

[219] Mark 14:58

[220] Mark 15:1

Politics in itself can be oppressive, especially for those who don't fit in with the way that the majority happens to be. You can find yourself persecuted, deported, even executed, on being labeled a subversive, a dissident, a threat to the establishment. When you combined politics and religion, and the religion is a system of judging and condemning, then you give religion a power that can be used against anyone it can label as being wrong. The whole of religion turning Jesus over to the representative of politics is symbolic of the corrupt system that must be done away with if things are ever to get any better. Jesus ran counter-culture to both religion and politics.

> My lovers and my friends stand aloof from my sore; and my kinsmen stand afar off. They also that seek after my life lay snares for me: and they that seek my hurt speak mischievous things, and imagine deceits all the day long. But I, as a deaf man, heard not; and I was **as a dumb man that openeth not his mouth**. Thus I was as a man that heareth not, **and in whose mouth are no reproofs**. For in thee, O LORD, do I hope: thou wilt hear, O Lord my God. For I said, Hear me, lest otherwise they should rejoice over me: when my foot slippeth, they magnify themselves against me.[221]

There is nothing to say, nothing that can be said. They have their agenda. They have their tradition to uphold and defend. They have already labeled and sentenced you in their mind. You just have to remember that you are linked to something greater than them, something they cannot understand in you, something they cannot overpower in you.

> Woe to their soul, for they have devised an evil counsel against themselves, saying against themselves, **Let us bind the just, for he is burdensome to us**: therefore shall they eat the fruits of their works.[222]

They had to bind Jesus, put Jesus away, hand Jesus over. Either that or they had to deal with Jesus, follow his message and reform their entire way of thinking, their vision, their values, their judgmental attitude, their xenophobic isolationism, their limiting the "word of God" to their own texts and their own interpretations. This was too great of a burden for them. Much easier to just gag Jesus, tie him up, prevent him from saying anything more or doing anything more.

---

[221] Psalm 38:11-16

[222] Isaiah 3:10 (LXX) (Brenton translation)

> Jesus answered, **My kingdom is not of this world**: if my kingdom were of this world, then would my servants fight, **that I should not be delivered to the Jews**: but now is my kingdom not from hence. Pilate therefore said unto him, Art thou a king then? Jesus answered, Thou sayest that I am a king. To this end was I born, and for this cause came I into the world, that I should bear witness unto the truth. Every one that is of the truth heareth my voice.[223]

If it was just another religious war, the one new religion could battle it out with the old existing religion. There could be crusades of Christians against Jews, kingdom against kingdom. Jesus is not a replacement religion of this world. Some may make it become that in the future, but that is not the intention. Jesus is king of another dimension, ruler of something distinct from the religion and politics of this world.

> Then the presidents and princes sought to find occasion against Daniel concerning **the kingdom**; but they could find none occasion nor fault; forasmuch as he was faithful, **neither was there any error or fault found in him**. Then said these men, We shall not find any occasion against this Daniel, except we find it against him concerning **the law of his God**.[224]

What could any non-biased government have against Jesus? He preaches peace and forgiveness, charity and good works. He represents the highest concept of What Is as a direct-connection channel. It is only when politics gets corrupted by religion that it takes on that fundamentalist stench of judgmental condemnation of whatever the religion fears.

> But the chief priests moved the people, that he should rather release **Barabbas** unto them.[225]

The choice was presented. Barabbas, the "son of the fathers", was intent on insurrection, murder, the revolutionary war method of obtaining change. Jesus promoted the love of the enemies, working for peace, embracing diversity, forgiveness, which sounded weak and unbefitting their imagined God-given duties to fight the holy war. They made their choice. Condemn the silly peace-talking pacifist. Go with the revolutionaries with a definite plan for

---

[223] John 18:36-37

[224] Daniel 6:4-5

[225] Mark 15:11

change. The anti-war subversives have to be silenced. They are undermining the rallying of the people in support of the revolution.

Saoul

Andy found a tradition where others had thought along the same lines as Mark.

> Howbeit we speak wisdom among them that are perfect: yet not the wisdom of this world, nor of the princes of this world, that come to nought: But we speak the wisdom of God in a mystery, even the hidden wisdom, which God ordained before the world unto our glory: Which none of the princes of this world knew: for had they known it, they would not have crucified the Lord of glory.[226]

The ideas were from a traveling teacher named Saoul that passed through Pella on the way to Arabia. He was an odd sort of man, but with a sincere passion for his ideas. He didn't care to hear any of the stories from Mary or Simon, but he was interesting in comparing notes with Mark as to which scriptural references could be applied to Jesus, who he simply called Christ. In his version, the "princes of this world" was code for a political structure beyond that of the Romans, beyond earthly political rulers like Pilatos. The princes were the archons, the angelic or god forces that haunt and inhabit the unseen realm that oversees and connects us all. The world was aion, which means something more than just the planet we stand on. Aion is our age, our reality, or realm, our place in the grand scheme of it all. The hidden wisdom is the answer to overcoming the archons. The "Lord" has come to reveal this wisdom, but the archons could not understand and thus they misunderstood him, rejected him, killed him. It was just like Mark's vision of the death of Jesus in Jerusalem, but the place and time were more obscure, the event living in the realm of pure myth.

---

[226] 1 Corinthians 2:6-8

> Wherein in time past ye walked according to the course of this world, according to the prince of the power of the air, the spirit that now worketh in the children of disobedience: Among whom also we all had our conversation in times past in the lusts of our flesh, fulfilling the desires of the flesh and of the mind; and were by nature the children of wrath, even as others. But God, who is rich in mercy, for his great love wherewith he loved us, Even when we were dead in sins, hath quickened us together with Christ, (by grace ye are saved;) And hath raised us up together, and made us sit together in heavenly places in Christ *Jesus*:[227]

For Saoul, there was a force to deal with that was stronger than earthly religion and earthly politics. This world (kosmos) was seen to be ruled by a prince (archon). He used the Greek word kosmos, which is a word expressing the overall arrangement of the universe, the cosmic order. Christ was seen to be a gift of grace from the merciful God that was beyond the cosmic archon. Now what was unclear to Andy was whether Saoul made the equation of the "cosmic archon" with the "God" of the Jerusalem Temple Jews. He meant to ask, but Saoul left Pella as quickly as he had arrived.

> But as it is written, Eye hath not seen, nor ear heard, neither have entered into the heart of man, the things which God hath prepared for them that love him. But God hath revealed them unto us by his Spirit: for the Spirit searcheth all things, yea, the deep things of God. For what man knoweth the things of a man, save the spirit of man which is in him? even so the things of God knoweth no man, but the Spirit of God. Now we have received, not the spirit of the world, but the spirit which is of God; that we might know the things that are freely given to us of God.[228]

The "spirit of the world" was the cosmic archon that could only be defeated in our lives by its replacement with the Spirit of God, which Andy took to mean the same thing as the Holy Spirit that they had been experiencing and discussing for some time now. This brought the conflict, the revolution, the change, the transformation, into another realm entirely. While the Jewish revolutionaries were fighting with tangible swords to defeat enemies with blood and muscles and weapons, the Jesus revolutionaries were fighting with spiritual forces that controlled and manipulated thoughts

---

[227] Ephesians 2:2-6

[228] 1 Corinthians 2:9-12

Some things you have to poison, weed out, remove, while you feed other things, plant, organize. Completion is not just a collection of learnings, it is also a collection of unlearning the wrong ways of thinking. Life without death? New beginning without the end of the old order? If you don't question the way things have always been, you don't look for new answers to how things could be. And once you have the new vision, the new intention, the promoted awareness of the way things are, you don't go back to the unenlightened way of thinking. That is now gone, Saoul explained. Washed out and hung up to dry! Left as a memorial of what used to matter, of how it used to be.

> God forbid. How shall we, that are dead to sin, live any longer therein? Know ye not, that so many of us as were baptized into *Jesus* Christ were baptized into his death? Therefore we are buried with him by baptism into death: that like as Christ was raised up from the dead by the glory of the Father, even so we also should walk in newness of life. For if we have been planted together in the likeness of his death, we shall be also in the likeness of his resurrection: Knowing this, that our old man is crucified with him, that the body of sin might be destroyed, that henceforth we should not serve sin. For he that is dead is freed from sin. Now if we be dead with Christ, we believe that we shall also live with him:[229]

There is a sense of symbolism at play here, of the death of Jesus being a pattern for crucifying a part of ourselves that we no longer want to carry around with us, destroying it, being dead to it and having it be dead to our new way of life.

> And they that are Christ's have crucified the flesh with the affections and lusts.[230]

The Greek word stauroo can be crucified, but it also means staked, held in place, controlled, nailed down. It could be translated as "trashed" and the meaning would become clearer. While the ignorant archons "trashed" the "Lord of glory",[231] the enlightened Christians "trash" the mind game controls of the archons that come with living in "the flesh with affections and lusts".

---

[229] Romans 6:2-8

[230] Galatians 5:24

[231] 1 Corinthians 2:8

> O foolish Galatians, who hath bewitched you, that ye should not obey the truth, before whose eyes *Jesus* Christ hath been evidently set forth, crucified among you?[232]

This "crucified among you" presented the event of the crucifixion in a way that transcends any one specific place or time. It was an evident perpetual sacrifice being made.

> For I through the law am dead to the law, that I might live unto God. I am crucified with Christ: nevertheless I live; yet not I, but Christ liveth in me: and the life which I now live in the flesh I live by the faith of the Son of God, who loved me, and gave himself for me. I do not frustrate the grace of God: for if righteousness come by the law, then Christ is dead in vain.[233]

This being "crucified with Christ" was the conversion event for the Christian mindset. The "Son of God" was given to experience a "death" that we all must partake of, according to Saoul.

> But God forbid that I should glory, save in the cross of our Lord *Jesus* Christ, by whom the world is crucified unto me, and I unto the world.[234]

The world (kosmos) is crucified (stauroo) to me and I to the world. This gives such a powerful image that at the same time cannot be taken literally. Understood symbolically, the obvious is that "Jesus Christ" has such meaning that the values of the kosmos are considered trash to us and we are considered to be worthless in the attempts to mind control by the normal concerns and cravings of "worldly" minded people.

> Jesus came to crucify the world.[235]

These thoughts sat in Mark's mind while he gelled together his passion play of Jesus in Jerusalem being rejected by religion and politics. In the same way that pesher studies of

---

[232] Galatians 3:1

[233] Galatians 2:19-21

[234] Galatians 6:14

[235] Philip 63.24

ancient texts could reveal truths at many different levels at the same time, so Mark wanted his "good story" to have messages pop out from various perspectives.

> And they clothed him with **purple**, and platted a crown of thorns, and put it about his head, And began to salute him, Hail, King of the Jews![236]

There is something powerful about grounding the story, giving it a place and time, giving it human interaction and response. To acknowledge, but only in a mocking sort of way, to respect but in jest, lay at the heart of Judaism, that submersed thread of hope from which Jesus had been extracted. It wasn't the message that the revolutionaries wanted to hear at the present. The mocking takes on a deeper meaning when seen through the failure of the revolution. Was this the dark shadow side of Jesus? His alter ego was this Son of David Messiah figure to sit in victory after the defeat of the Romans. Here the Romans mocked him, or mocked the concept of "Son of David Messiah" that they took him to represent.

Here comes Simon the serene in from the country, arriving in Jerusalem for the first time, here you go – carry the cross of the Son of David Messiah to the place of the skull. Put the delusionary ambition to sweet eternal sleep.[237] He really can't be crucified without your help, dear Simon. You have to want it to end.

What does this story of death have to do with the Jesus that Simon had known? What does this story have to do with walking on the water, with plenty of food, with calming storms, with escaping violent situations? Each is but part of a larger story that has to be told, Mark assured him.

> To the swine he will throw acorns, to the cattle he will throw barley and chaff and grass, to the dogs he will throw bones. To the slaves he will give only the elementary lessons, to the children he will give the complete instruction.[238]

When the "Answer" is out there, it cannot flow, it cannot help. Lots of blind faith and futile hope later and Christ is still not flying out of the sky on the dust clouds of angelic war horses. When "they" have so defined and confined and limited Christ, over-prophesized him out of a possibility of starring in his own role, the "Answer" must die if it is to come back to any

---

[236] Mark 15:17-18

[237] Mark 15:21-22

[238] Philip 81.9-14

meaningful life. This is the dance of out and in that Mark envisioned for his epic message for the world. Simon denies and runs away. Simon finds himself carrying the very cross that is to kill his very "Answer". In the end, Simon sees his "Jesus" alive in a way that he could never have lived apart from having died. Jude also goes through the dance of the story, but with his own roles to play. The obsession with the money bag, the betrayal, the repenting of the betrayal, the throwing back of the money, the doubts about "Jesus" being alive, all climaxed in his one hand-felt touch of the resurrected Lord. Mary had her part in the dance as well, the anointing in preparation for death, the faithful vigil beside the cross, the first on the scene at the dawning of the new day, the first to see and speak with "Jesus" in his resurrected state.

> Then he brought me to the door of the gate of the LORD'S house which was toward the north; and, behold, **there sat women weeping for Tammuz**. Then said he unto me, **Hast thou seen this, O son of man? turn thee yet again, and thou shalt see greater abominations than these**.[239]

It was part of the mysteries for there to be the death of the god-man hero. What happens when the god-man hero story is told in the context of Judaism? It is the very feeling of emotional connection that is at the same time surpassing of and a confrontational denial of the old religion. It is an abomination and yet a release. It is destruction and clearing the foundation for new erections. What did it poetically mean for Jesus to die in Jerusalem as a sign, as a triggering event for the beginning of the end?

> Therefore thus saith the Lord GOD; As the vine tree among the trees of the forest, which I have given to the fire for fuel, so will I give the inhabitants of Jerusalem. And I will set my face against them; they shall go out from one fire, and another fire shall devour them; and ye shall know that I am the LORD, when I set my face against them. And I will make the land desolate, because they have committed a trespass, saith the Lord GOD.[240]

Jesus provided the definition of the trespass, the reason for cosmic justice to be served for Jerusalem. They harvested what they planted.[241] They rejected and judged and condemned their only hope. It was a thought that was circulating around the Great Sea in the aftermath of the failed Jewish revolutionary war. Mark just connected it to the spiritual symbol of the

---

[239] Ezekiel 8:14-15

[240] Ezekiel 15:6-8

[241] Galatians 6:7

anti-war movement, Jesus. This told their story in a way that could not have been otherwise. Simon understood this in the end.

> And the kings of the earth, and the great men, and the rich men, and the chief captains, and the mighty men, and every bondman, and every free man, hid themselves in the dens and in the rocks of the mountains; And said to the mountains and rocks, Fall on us, and hide us from the face of him that sitteth on the throne, and from the wrath of the Lamb: For the great day of his wrath is come; and who shall be able to stand?[242]

The wrath of the Messianic Lamb to come faded into the victory of the Roman legions, pushing the last of the revolutionaries into hiding in caves and tunnels, fleeing for their lives and dying.

> And when the sixth hour was come, there was darkness over the whole land until the ninth hour.[243]

The whole play of light and darkness, of good and evil, of law and sin, of the duality of drawing a line down the center and separating the sheep from the goats was riding on the vision of the ultimate war and the ultimate defeat of the children of darkness by the children of light. It was to be the dawning of a new day, a day brighter than ever before, with all light and no darkness, all good and no evil. That day was at hand in the eternal now as Jesus in his Messianic Son of David persona hung nailed to the cross. And for all the expectations of what it would be like, it was the opposite. The sun refused to shine – at all. It was a total eclipse of the hopes and dreams of those who wanted to purify the world of those different. In the darkness, they all looked the same, saint and sinner, rich and poor, young and old, local or foreigner. Darkness, that great equalizer. The great inspirer:

> Shall not the land tremble for this, and every one mourn that dwelleth therein? And it shall rise up wholly as a flood; and it shall be cast out and drowned, as by the flood of Egypt. And it shall come to pass in that day, saith the Lord GOD, **that I will cause the sun to go down at noon, and I will darken the earth in the clear day**: And I will turn your feasts into mourning, and all your songs into lamentation; and I will bring up sackcloth upon all loins, and baldness upon every head; **and I will make it as the mourning of an only son**, and the end thereof as a bitter day. Behold, the days come,

---

[242] Revelation 6:15-17

[243] Mark 15:33

> saith the Lord GOD, that I will send a famine in the land, not a famine of bread, nor a thirst for water, but of hearing the words of the LORD: And they shall wander from sea to sea, and from the north even to the east, they shall run to and fro to seek the word of the LORD, and shall not find it.[244]

There was a Jesus saying that went something like: If you want to see the most star lights, you must place yourself at night in a place that is very dark.[245]

> And the light shineth in darkness; and the darkness comprehended it not.[246]

The final gasp of the Son of David Messiah, dying on the Roman cross, represented the final words of most of the revolutionaries. Why did God not come to their aid? Why did God allow the Romans to win? Why did God not send the Messiah with the clouds of dust rising up from an angelic host of apocalyptic horses? Why did God not rain down fire and brimstone from heaven and help the chosen people regain control of the promised land?

> And at the ninth hour Jesus cried with a loud voice, saying, Eloi, Eloi, lama sabachthani? Which is, being interpreted, **My God, my God, why hast thou forsaken me?**[247]

The most visible sign of the defeat of the Jewish revolutionaries was the absence of the Temple in Jerusalem. It had been ripped apart, leveled, demolished from top to bottom. This void stood as representing the old religion that had its heart ripped out, that could not imagine to lift itself back up and continue. The Temple represented the presence of God, the connection of God to the people, the Holy of Holies link between the divine and the mundane. When the Son of David Messiah dream died, the link was severed.

> And the veil of the temple was rent in twain from the top to the bottom.[248]

---

[244] Amos 8:8-12

[245] Dialogue of the Saviour 14

[246] John 1:5

[247] Mark 15:34

[248] Mark 15:38

> And the temple of God was opened in heaven, and there was seen in his temple the ark of his testament: and there were lightnings, and voices, and thunderings, and an earthquake, and great hail.[249]

Christians liked the word "new" and the thoughts that came to mind were involving a "new" Jerusalem with a "new" Temple that had a "new" Ark that held for us a "new" Testament. The "new" Jerusalem was not an earthly city, it was the home of the "real" Jesus. The "new" Temple was that inner space of overlapping realms, with its "new" Ark of Jesus allowing us direct-connection to What Is. The "old" Testament was for a select few priests to enter a human made Temple and reenact supposedly ancient rituals that at one time might have plugged some real person into some real metaphysical experience. The "new" Testament was for everyone, for all of us, being played out in our inner temples, creating a living tradition that we can pass on and share.

Resurrection

> "And the goddess answered, 'Ulysses, noble son of Laertes, you shall none of you stay here any longer if you do not want to, but there is another journey which you have got to take before you can sail homewards. You must go to the house of Hades and of dread Proserpine to consult the ghost of the blind Theban prophet Teiresias whose reason is still unshaken. To him alone has Proserpine left his understanding even in death, but the other ghosts flit about aimlessly.' "I was dismayed when I heard this. I sat up in bed and wept, and would gladly have lived no longer to see the light of the sun, but presently when I was tired of weeping and tossing myself about, I said, 'And who shall guide me upon this voyage- for the house of Hades is a port that no ship can reach.'[250]

---

[249] Revelation 11:19

[250] Homer: Odyssey 10

Jesus descended into hell before he resurrected. In Greek mythology, hell is the house of Hades. Before Ulysses could return to reclaim his house, he had to take a side trip though Hades, through Sheol. While the Son of David Messiah was to be propelled to the brink of victory and world domination, the Elect One was pushed to death, to destruction, to snares of an inscrutable abyss:

> For he delivered the physical life of his Elect One from the hands of death; and he redeemed his Holy One from destruction. And he saved me from the snares of Sheol; and brought me forth from the abyss that is inscrutable.[251]

This was a key point in the great reversal mindset that Mark was weaving into his story. Life and death are not what they appear. Greatness is destined to be great; defeat is only a small setback, even the defeat of being dead. The eternal part of us cannot kill or be killed in the wars that can only destroy the body.

> Those who say that the Lord died first and then rose up are in error, for he rose up first and then died. If one does not first attain the resurrection he will not die.[252]

Death is the release, the goal, the escape, the accomplishment of shedding off that which cannot follow. The miracle of Jesus is not that he died and then came back to the same type of life that he had before he died. The miracle is that he attained, or demonstrated to us how to attain, a resurrected state of being, a new identification, an ascended mindset, and then thrust himself through death in order to purify the transition. What lives after the experience is not the same as what was put to death. Flesh and blood do not make it to the Kingdom. You may still look down and see the body, but you are now wearing it, using it, not identifying with it. You are something more, something eternal, something that will survive any death that comes your way. I shall be released, and what would "released" be if you find yourself trapped to a bag of bones for eternity? No, that is not what we meant by the talks of resurrection, but there are many since then that have come to misunderstand. It is the spirit that gains Life, the flesh profits nothing from the experience.[253]

---

[251] Psalm 153:2-3

[252] Philip 56.15-19

[253] John 6:63

> But the souls of the righteous are in the hand of God, and no torment will ever touch them. **In the eyes of the foolish they seemed to have died, and their departure was thought to be an affliction, and their going from us to be their destruction; but they are at peace. For though in the sight of men they were punished, their hope is full of immortality.** Having been disciplined a little, they will receive great good, because God tested them and found them worthy of himself; like gold in the furnace he tried them, and like a sacrificial burnt offering he accepted them. **In the time of their visitation they will shine forth, and will run like sparks through the stubble. They will govern nations and rule over peoples, and the Lord will reign over them for ever.** Those who trust in him will understand truth, and the faithful will abide with him in love, because grace and mercy are upon his elect, and he watches over his holy ones.[254]

The book of Enoch was popular among Jewish sects that looked for something to maintain a hope in. Who was the Elect One? He was not anything that they had been looking for or trying to define or create or imagine. The Nazarenes saw in this hope a portrait of their Jesus, and rightfully so:

> In those days, Sheol will return all the deposits which she had received and hell will give back all that which it owes. And he shall choose the righteous and the holy ones from among the risen dead, for the day when they shall be selected and saved has arrived. In those days, the **Elect One** shall sit on my throne, and from the conscience of his mouth shall come out all the secrets of wisdom, for the Lord of the Spirits has given them to him and glorified him. In those days, mountains shall dance like rams; and the hills shall leap like kids satiated with milk. And the faces of all the angels in heaven shall glow with joy, because on that day **the Elect One has arisen**. And the earth shall rejoice; and the righteous ones shall dwell upon her and the elect ones shall walk upon her.[255]
>
> And these measurements shall reveal all the secrets of the depths of the earth, those who have been destroyed in the desert, those who have been devoured by the wild beasts, and those who have been eaten by the fish of the sea. So that they all return and find hope in the day of the Elect One. For there is no one who perishes before the Lord of the Spirits, and no one who should perish.[256]

---

[254] Wisdom of Solomon 3:1-9

[255] 1 Enoch 51:1-5

[256] 1 Enoch 61:5

This was an important theme to Saoul. In his way of thinking, resurrection was key. His idea of "Christ risen" was to take hold of Christianity as "the" symbol for what it stood for. It was radical, rooted, down to the depths of the ancestry of all of humanity, of Adam, and of the Son of Adam. It was being born into a life that has to end in death as compared to a sense of dying to a life that leaves you feeling eternally alive. Was Mark going to end the story for the reader to decide? He reasoned that each initiate must find the risen Jesus in his own way. Some, like little Jude, will have to reach out and touch the ghost of Jesus past.[257] Blessed are those who can know of the living Jesus without having to see and touch anything at all.

Now if Christ be preached that he rose from the dead, how **say some among you that there is no resurrection of the dead**? But if there be no resurrection of the dead, then is Christ not risen: And if Christ be not risen, then is our preaching vain, and your faith is also vain. Yea, and we are found false witnesses of God; because we have testified of God that he raised up Christ: whom he raised not up, if so be that the dead rise not. For if the dead rise not, then is not Christ raised: And if Christ be not raised, your faith is vain; ye are yet in your sins. Then they also which are fallen asleep in Christ are perished. If in this life only we have hope in Christ, we are of all men most miserable. But now is Christ risen from the dead, and become the firstfruits of them that slept. For since by man came death, by man came also the resurrection of the dead. For as in Adam all die, even so in Christ shall all be made alive. But every man in his own order: Christ the firstfruits; afterward they that are Christ's at his coming. Then cometh the end, when he shall have delivered up the kingdom to God, even the Father; when he shall have put down all rule and all authority and power. For he must reign, till he hath put all enemies under his feet. The last enemy that shall be destroyed is death.[258]

The empty tomb. To expect to see the remains of a beaten and tortured body, lifeless and hopeless, and then to see only a youthful living man dressed in clean white with a sense of serene reassurance on his face and in his voice.

The Rulers thought that it was by their own power and will that they were doing what they did, but the Holy Spirit in secret was accomplishing everything through them as it wished. Truth, which existed since the beginning, is sown everywhere. And many see it being sown, but few are they who see it being reaped.[259]

---

[257] John 20:24-25

[258] 1 Corinthians 15:12-26

[259] Philip 55.14-22

The death is a big public bonfire crowded event. The resurrection is a private viewing for those who have eyes to see and ears to hear. Mary gazed into the bright eyes of the youth with one of those jolting moments of change. She saw the future, glaring with the light of eternity, of hope for peace and sanity and compassion to rule the hearts of those who can experience the new life. Like the cycles of days and moons and seasons, the old man of the old year giving way to the young child of the new year, so too it echoed through the turning of the new age in which Pisces dawned after the lamb of Aries was slain. A new age brings new hope. She was happy she had lived to see it dawn.

> And **entering into the sepulchre**, they saw a **young man sitting** on the right side, clothed in a long white garment; and they were affrighted. And he saith unto them, Be not affrighted: Ye seek **Jesus the Nazarite**, which was crucified: **he is risen**; he is not here: behold the place where they laid him.[260]

This is the way Mark ended the story, with the graphic image of Jesus renewed, young again, strong again, pure and clean again. There were those who read the story, Jake included, that thought that the young man was an angel, but it was obvious from the way Mark thought and wove ideas together that this was the resurrected Jesus.

---

[260] Mark 16:5-6

Jesus Gnosis
Story of Simon
By Philip

As a holder of this book, you are hereby invited to join an online discussion group about the subjects and issues raised by this book:

Yahoo Groups: http://groups.yahoo.com/group/JesusGnosis

Other books by Thomas Ragland

The Noble Eightfold Path of Christ:
Jesus Teaches the Dharma of Buddhism

ISBN-10: 1412000130
ISBN-13: 978-1412000130
ASIN: B0027G6XT2 (Amazon Kindle Edition)
Yahoo Groups: http://groups.yahoo.com/group/Christ_And_Buddha

The ancient Theravada Buddhist canonical suttas, the beloved Mahayana Buddhist sutras, and the Tao Te Ching have been lovingly mined for concepts and realizations. These ideas resonate with the heart of the teachings of Jesus the Nazarene as preserved in the Christian gospels.

Buddha Turns the Kabbalah Wheel:
Jewish Buddhist Resonance from a Christian Gnostic Perspective

ISBN-10: 1412064619
ISBN-13: 978-1412064613
ASIN: B000QEC8FK (Amazon Kindle Edition)
Yahoo Groups: http://groups.yahoo.com/group/Buddha_Turns_The_Kabbalah_Wheel

The words that make up the sefirot of the Kabbalah are present in the original Hebrew version of the Bible. Letting these words be defined by their usage in the Hebrew scriptures leaves us with an exacting scholarly definition of each.

For the purpose of blending Jewish thought with Buddhist thought, the sefirot are presented as a wheel. What is amazing in this presentation is that the sefirot then line up perfectly with Buddha's Noble Eightfold Path as the circumference and Buddhism's Three Jewels as the hub of the Kabbalah Wheel.